CHRIS LOWRY

Big Easy Witch – The Marshal of Magic

Contents

1

CHAPTER ONE

BIG EASY WITCH

"It's beginning to look a lot like Witchmas. Everywhere you turn."

"Do you mind?"

"What?"

"You're humming?"

"I was not."

"You were. You were humming a Christmas tune."

"It's not Christmas," Elvis curled his lip as well as his namesake.

"That's not the most annoying part."

"It was more annoying than singing Christmas tunes out of season? I am agog."

"You are a ghost. A ghost changing the lyrics to Christmas tunes. I'm allowed to arrest you for that."

"Do you have corporeal cuffs?" he held out his wrists.

They looked solid, if wispy, a paler version of the intellectual I once called a friend. Still called a friend since he was tethered to me by some unseen form of justice, or crazy karma.

"You said Witchmas."

"A Witch mass," he mused.

If you've never seen a ghost muse it's almost as funny as it sounds. First, he looked pensive, as if he was searching his memory banks for what a witch mass might be.

He didn't have to tell me. I knew.

I'd seen one in Germany in World War II, the final war to end all wars since all we engaged in since were police actions in regional conflicts. That coven, like this one, had been doing demon work.

Back then the Sidhe were involved, and part of the peace process was they would no longer interfere in the matters of men.

I know the Sidhe don't' have short memories.

They're practically immortal and hold contracts, accords and promises as sacred.

Which meant either this coven had gone rogue and scattered thirteen demons around the United States, or the worse option.

The worse option by its definition was really bad.

Really, really bad.

"I need a beer," I sighed.

Elvis perked up with that one, then his face deflated, the pensive look replaced by utter dejection.

"I can't taste beer, Marshal."

If ghosts could cry, he would be.

Elvis moaned instead. It was a mournful lonesome sound that sent a series of goosebumps dancing up my spine and made me shiver.

"I liked the Christmas carol better," I shivered again.

"Sorry," he said. "I would tell you it's all in your head, because it is. Literally. We're connected now."

"You'll have to tell me more about it later. Right now, let's get some evidence and find out where to start hunting for these witches."

2

CHAPTER TWO

The crime scene as I called it was empty. Barren. Evidence of the ritual that brought demons back to this plane was erased, the alter destroyed and made to look like a pile of construction rocks.

I could feel the power of the ley line pulsing below me, a steady thrum of energy like standing next to a buried powerline.

"1.21 Gigawatts," I muttered as I stepped through the tingle again.

"Great Scott!" Elvis drawled behind me.

"I can't find anything," I confessed.

"Strong magic is afoot," he said. "And someone is cleaning up after it."

Which meant we either still had someone in Memphis doing Witch dirty work, or the purveyor of evil had done the deed and split.

I was opting for split.

Memphis isn't my hometown, since I roam all over the East in service of the Marshals, but I spent a lot of time there. Enough that magic users knew it was a home base, or sorts.

Technically, my home base was a beat up pick up truck with an eight foot bed.

It was warded, had a place to sleep in the back and a locked metal toolbox full of implements and instruments.

Mobile, discreet, and under a permanent shield when I wasn't around it.

I sometimes even parked it by the river, just so I could spout out the line, "In a truck down by the river," to anyone who would offer a laugh in exchange.

I wasn't homeless. I was living the dirtbag life, ready to travel at a second's notice.

Plus, I had a credit card from the Judge that was black and could get me into any hotel in the world, no matter the star rating.

When I whipped that sucker out, eyes got wide and the obsequious sucking up began.

"Where are we going?" Elvis asked.

I stopped on the edge of the construction site and stared at the flowing water of the mighty river the new neighborhood was perched on.

Something about the tug of the current drew my eyes, and I let them wander to the South.

"You would think the Judge would poof us where we needed to be," I said to the ghost at my shoulder in a distracted voice.

"He knew you had me."

"Yeah, but you haven't figured it out yet."

"I will."

The wind picked up, floating trash paper around us in a swirling tumble of acrobatic flight. An aluminum soda can rolled and rattled across the asphalt and tumbled into a rock strewn ditch.

A second can fetched up against my hiking boots and held there.

I bent to pick it up.

A yellow can of chicory coffee from a world famous establishment in New Orleans. I looked up from the can and saw I was still facing south.

"You couldn't just have said it out loud?" I shouted at the clouds on the horizon.

"Said what?" Elvis asked. "I don't have to talk out loud. You can hear me in your mind."

"I wasn't talking to you."

"Then who were you talking to?" the Elvis impersonator said in a DeNiro voice. "I'm the only one here. You must be talking to me."

I held out the can with the faded cover to show him our destination.

"The Judge wants us to go to New Orleans."

"You think?" said the ghost and his eyes got a faraway look in them.

"That feels right," he said after a moment. "Didn't we do something in the Big Easy once?"

I nodded, but he didn't see me. He was staring toward the south, following the curve of the river and trying like hell to remember.

"We did," I told him. "The medium."

He nodded, like someone who couldn't recall, but knew they should.

"It's getting a little misty up here," he tapped a long slender finger against his temple.

"But Hannah is still there, right? Hannah can help."

Hannah wasn't the medium, but she could help. At least he remembered her name.

"Hannah," I told him and his face lit up in a smile, happy he had pulled that at least from the cobwebs of his memory.

"Nothing to it but to get to it," he lifted a lip. "Takin care of TCB."

I climbed into the truck and let him float through the open window to settle on the other side of the bench seat.

"It's a long drive," he said.

I fired up the trusty old straight six and dropped the gearshift on the column to D.

"Nine hour drive, or five hours on a train," I told him. "We'll take the City of New Orleans to the city of New Orleans."

That earned another tight ghost smile.

I sighed.

What good was a watcher without the knowledge they provided. Pretty soon, Elvis would just be haunting me, and I needed to find out how to stop it. The haunting and the memory loss.

3

CHAPTER THREE

I felt a subtle tug of magic.

I blinked.

He blanched.

Neither of us were supposed to be able to do that.

My beautiful new friend was a vampire and I just caught him trying to entrance a human.

Not just an offense, but offensive.

I slid the coat open to show him the badge on my belt.

"That what you're talking about?"

"You can't smell him?"

I sniffed.

The air smelled like spices and sand, cinnamon and cardamom, an exotic blend that was sweet and cloying and at the same time covered the stench of something dead.

People smell it all the time and mistake it for roadkill.

"You can?"

"Ghosts can't smell Marshal," Elvis explained. "But he doesn't have an aura."

I blinked into magic sight, that tiny shift in the spectrum that lets magic users see things most normal humans don't.

"Pardon me," the vampire begged in a cultured voice.

He could have been from Georgia the state, or Georgia the country, but either way he was far from home and riding a train to New Orleans.

"I didn't realize you were the Marshal."

I tilted my head to one side and studied him.

"If I had been human, you'd be feeding right now."

Technically, I am human, but who shares that sort of intel with a bloodsucker.

"It's a habit," he offered a hand. "Hello Marshal, I am Claude."

A pretense of peace.

Vampires have been around pretty much since the beginning of time.

Some folks debated that they were aliens, sent here to feed on the human cattle and at one time had been the overlords of fallen empires.

If that was the case, those empires might have declined because their rulers were eating them.

Some debated that the Vampire was created by Jesus when he resurrected Lazarus. I'd have to ask the Judge since rumor held he was around at the time.

As far as I knew, Vamps had been here forever. They worked with the Sidhe a long time ago, and announced their independence millennia ago.

Still, they weren't supposed to feed on unwilling humans.

There were laws against that.

"I wasn't going to partake," Claude said. "Call it my predator nature. I cannot help it."

It was trying to hypnotize me.

I wasn't sure I believed him.

"Why are you on a train?"

"How else would one travel?" he looked around the empty car.

We were the only two passengers in this section of the train, the seats around us empty due to a low level vibration I cast that made people uncomfortable so they would give me room.

I should have noticed when he sat across from me.

Chalk it up to being preoccupied with worse things.

Thought what's worse than a hungry vampire seducing you for your blood, I don't know.

Demons, sure, but they were out there, and he was in here.

I realized there were a lot of empty seats around us.

Very private. And vampires were fast.

If Claude decided to take a bite, just a nibble to see what magic blood tasted like, I wasn't sure if I could stop him.

He shifted forward and the tip of my finger sparked.

I watched the glowing ring around his eyes contract and he held up a hand.

"I mean you no harm, Marshal."

I was sitting across the aisle from a vampire.

Anyone might have guessed by the pale, almost blue color of his skin, the dark gothic outfit favored by so many, or the tips of the sharp canines that left an indentation in his purple blood colored lips.

Except me.

I guessed by magic, as in the absence of his lifeforce and the addition of a glamour.

The glamour was subtle, enough to make people overlook him and pass by his seat.

But it made me stare.

Which he noticed.

He licked his lip with a worm colored tongue and bared his fangs, a threat.

I slid my coat to one side and showed him the badge.

The Nosferatu don't have a panic reflex that cause their pupils to dilate. That part of their brain stops working once they die.

But the skin around his eyes tightened, and the sharp intake of breath was loud enough for me to hear.

"Not just any geek off the street," I told him.

That earned me a look from a stern looking school marm type sitting at the end of the cart. It must have looked like I was talking to an empty seat to her.

She harrumphed with righteous indignation, and even though we were the only two people in the train car, she bustled out of the other door like she was late for a Church meeting.

"She did not appreciate you," the ghost of Elvis Rodriguez said over my shoulder.

Correction, only two live people.

Now down to one.

I sat across from the vamp.

"I am innocent of all wrong doing, Marshal," he said.

His voice was cultured, upper crust New England from the turn of the century.

The last one, not this one.

"Just riding the train, partner."

I wasn't a real cowboy, never had been. But the Marshal of the West had a thing about gunslingers, and I liked it too. Went with the title. At least I didn't wear a hat.

"Headed for the city of New Orleans?" he asked.

it wasn't an odd question. Quite normal for two riders on the train to ask of each other.

But there was something in the way he said it.

It's tough to read body language on bloodsuckers.

Since they're dead, they tend to hold themselves still, to the point of being statues.

I bet there were plenty of victims who stopped by what they thought was an interesting sculpture of marble before being turned into a tasty snack.

Tone though, can hold a world of meaning.

Ever heard someone say, "I don't like your tone."

His tone sent a little tiny shiver down my spine, like it was on the verge of being a threat.

One of my magical gifts is a little bit of pre-cog, which kept me alive more times than I care to count. His tone was making my warning bells go off like the Liberty Bell on July 2.

That's right, July 2 is the true Independence Day, even though we celebrate it on the 4th.

I cocked the tip of my finger in his direction.

Vampires were lightning fast.

Magic was actually lightning though, as fast as a thought process, at least when potions weren't involved.

The statue of a vamp pushed back in his seat, scooting further away from me, going out of his way to prove he wasn't a threat.

"You're not the first Marshal I've met," he said.

"Tonight?"

He smiled, but it was the grin of a predator upon meeting another, not a genuine emotion.

"Alas, this was many years ago. Your predecessor's mentor, if memory serves."

Vampires didn't forget, so his memory was just fine.

That meant he was a couple hundred years old, older than his accent led me to believe.

"What's in New Orleans?"

The smile dropped from his cheeks and he gazed out of the window. The soybean and cotton fields stretched out into the darkness on either side of the train, the black night and sparse landscape combining so that it was impossible to tell where one ended and the other began.

"I am meeting an old friend."

"LeStat?"

"That book," he sighed, even though breathing wasn't necessary. "Wonders for the tourist trade in an incredible town, but made a poor guide for those of my kind."

He crossed one leg over the other and rested a thin pale hand upon his knee.

"Would that it were more than fiction. Still," another sigh. "It was better than what Stoker did for us."

It might have been a pleasant conversation to pass the time as the train travelled South.

We both had a few years under our belts, some stories to share as we ate up the miles.

But it was not to be.

"Did you feel that?" Elvis whispered in my ear.

I did.

A different set of bells were clanging overtime and I glanced past the vampire through the window beyond.

Someone was performing a spell out there in the darkness.

A nasty spell with bad intent.

"Your familiar is correct," the vampire followed my look. "I regret we must wait until later to continue our conversation."

"We didn't get to talk much."

"Yet."

"Yet," I agreed and stood.

Vampires could see ghosts? I'd have to ask Elvis about that one. Maybe it was stored in his Watcher memories.

"Marshal," he tilted his head, canines till protruding.

"LeStat," I nodded back.

That earned a hint of a real smile.

"There is a convocation in New Orleans," he called after me as I moved toward the door of the railcar.

That made me stop.

"What kind of convocation?"

"The kind that could cause you trouble."

"Why tell me?"

"Your predecessor wasn't as kind to me as you've been," he said in a mysterious tone.

The kind that sent a shiver up my spine.

He meant the Marshal back up the line tried to blast him. Maybe even did blast him.

Since I didn't, he counted it as a kindness.

Who knows, he might have even liked our conversation.

I nodded.

It was a very cowboy thing to do.

Then I was out in the space between the railcars and forced the door open.

We were humming along at sixty miles per hour, which would have been scary if I didn't have magic to break my fall. I didn't think twice before jumping.

If I had, the fear might have stopped me.

Then I flicked my fingers and came to a running landing that left me up to my ankles in muck.

Magic. Good for jumping from moving trains.

Not so much on finding the right place to land.

Elvis floated next to me, feet out of the mud and water.

"Smooth move ex-lax," he curled his lip.

"I don't think that was a song of his."

"If it wasn't it should have been."

His eyes scanned the horizon and I followed his look. A soft orange glow indicated where something bad was going down.

"We could just poof over," he suggested.

But that didn't sound like the right thing to do.

You don't just appear in the middle of a spell. You could disrupt it, or worse. I mean, I'm not saying that's how I turned twelve demons of the zodiac loose on the world, but mistakes were made.

Still, if we were running, at least I could make it solid ground.

I shot a finger at the mud and froze it all the way to where the earth was dry and hard.

Then it took me two minutes to pry my feet out of the ice.

Elvis tried not to laugh while I grumbled.

He wasn't very good at it.

4

CHAPTER FOUR

There were legends of about young black men selling their souls to the devil so they could learn how to play the blues in Mississippi.

But those legends had a genesis in reality.

Except it wasn't the devil, it was a black magic woman, an old hoo doo priestess run out of New Orleans by Marie Laveau a few hundred years ago.

She ran far enough away to be safe and start up with a new community in the cotton fields close to the big muddy river.

I could feel it as we jumped off the moving train.

A leyline ran through here, north to Memphis. Scientists called it the New Madrid fault, because their logical minds couldn't wrap around magic.

Tell them about atoms and they would salivate.

Give them a conversation about quarks and they would dry

16

hump an encyclopedia about the so small sparks of life that made up atoms, the tiniest piece of matter that we could measure.

Mention magic and all that good will energy would evaporate like a raindrop on the dry Delta soil.

Scientists didn't believe in magic.

They needed facts.

Give them a fact that a leyline was a magnetic river of energy from where the Teutonic plates shifted together and they would accept one part of the equation and dismiss you as an idiot with the other.

"You feel it?" Elvis shivered next to me.

I told myself ghosts didn't shiver. Nothing to be afraid of once you're dead.

Didn't change the fact that his moaning voice sounded scared.

I wasn't going to ignore what was in front of me. I'm no scientist.

"It's bad. Can you tell what it is?"

He shook his head and had to repeat it when I looked over because I didn't hear him answer.

"There's history here," he told me. "Watchers."

He was my Watcher from Memphis, at least until I got him killed. Funny thing about his ghost was another fact I couldn't miss. Most ghosts who die traumatic deaths get tethered to a house, to a grave.

This man was killed by magic and the trauma tethered him to me.

It told me a little something about the way he died.

He had been thinking of me.

Cursing my name.

Not a great way to die.

And for me, not a great way to live. I had to do all my business with the ghost of an Elvis impersonator running color commentary.

It's nice to hear the word "Impressive" when you go to the bathroom for the first time, not so much when he makes fun of you for sitting down to pee.

I watched the watcher's face crinkle in concentration.

Another side effect of being dead was memory loss.

I figured it was the way of the dead moving on, forgetting about their life on this plane as they shift to the next.

For a ghost who made his living through knowledge, it was hell.

Or purgatory, since he was tied to me and I needed what he knew.

And he would have to watch me replace him, watch another Watcher take his place. It wasn't going to be fun or easy for both of us.

"A witch," he said and I tensed up.

Couldn't be one of the twelve I was chasing, since that was a new phenomenon, but he also said it like it was something I should have been familiar with.

"Which witch?"

He curled his upper lip.

"I told you about her, but you haven't been here."

Elvis told me a lot.

Even as a Watcher, he was also my friend. One of my only friends.

Alright, my only friend. I'm not a loser, just a little older than most of the people around me.

And more interested in magic than I am in whatever passes for news.

Or more interested in protecting people from bad magic, since that was my job.

With the occasional wit pro thrown in.

But if he told me about a river witch in the cotton fields, she wasn't doing enough bad magic to get my attention.

Until now.

There was a shield across the leyline.

A dome of energy designed to mask, diffuse and redirect anything that happened inside.

"Crap," I sighed.

The River Witch was not the old crone image I had built up in my mind. She was gorgeous, and powerful and right in the middle of sex magic, riding on top of a young black man lying in the dirt, a grimace of agony on his face, one hand gripping a battered blues guitar.

Sex magic was some of the most powerful magic in the land.

It also sent a small surge of jealousy through my gut because it had been awhile since anyone had pulled a pony trick on me.

The man was screaming, but it wasn't in pleasure.

That kind of magic pulls out the lifeforce.

Maybe even pulled it out through his dingus, hence the open mouth and thrown back head.

"You think that's why most blues players are so unlucky?" I asked the ghost as we approached the shimmering dome of energy. "They give up their life so they can get famous playing guitar."

"My namesake came to this crossroads," he told me. "I think he ended up being lucky."

"Maybe," I shrugged. "But he did die young. And his career flamed out when he went into the army."

Elvis punched my shoulder, but all I felt was a cold shiver run across my spine.

"He still had the gift, even if he was in a tank in Germany."

"Then why the comeback special?"

"It's all about marketing Marshal."

I tapped on the energy field and got a startled look from the witch.

Can't say that I blamed her. I would have been a little perturbed from coitus interruptus as well.

She flashed a hungry smile and held up one finger to tell me to wait a minute.

"Guess this is where the line starts."

"This is bad magic," Elvis told me. "And if she's expecting more to show up, then she's got a plan."

Was that it?

Were the witches in my territory emboldened by the screw up in Memphis? I was going to have to come up with a great wrestling name for it because referring to it as a screw up would just mess with my good luck magic further down the line.

You can't have negative vibes floating out there because they tend to attach to something and come back to haunt you.

The power of positive thinking is literally a thing.

Quantum physics is magic, and that's just how it works.

"What about Memphis Meltdown?" I said out loud as I pulled aside my coat.

"For what?" the ghost asked. "You might want to wait for that."

"Naming the ritual in Memphis?"

"Showing your badge?"

"Why?"

The ghost nodded to the witch.

"See what she's on?"

The black magic woman saw the badge I kept clipped to my belt and her eyes started to glow yellow.

"Dang, I see it now. You couldn't point that out before?"

"Hello, naked woman doing the nasty," said the ghost. "I didn't notice."

"Ghosts don't care about that," I said.

The witch stood up off the writhing naked man on the ground.

He rolled over on his side and curled in a fetal ball around the guitar.

Poor fellow did not look happy. He looked like he hurt, and bit off a little more than he could handle.

"Maybe other ghosts," said Elvis. "But I am a connoisseur of beautiful women. The Latin lover in me cannot help it."

She was gorgeous, even with yellow eyes. Muscular, shapely body standing in the dusty Mississippi topsoil, nothing hidden from our eyes.

"Okay Latin lover," I redirected him. "What's the symbol?"

"All magic has a toll, Marshal," he quirked up an eyebrow, waiting for me to get it.

I didn't.

I blame the naked woman.

She was very distracting.

"What always requires a toll?" Elvis asked, trying to keep exasperation from his voice and failing.

Crap.

There was one creature who loved a toll more than the expressway authority that liked to charge twenty five cents a mile on toll roads.

"Damn it."

"Yep," Elvis agreed.

The witch threw back her head and howled.

Then we felt it.

Even over the hum of the Leyline that ran all the way up to New Madrid.

Footsteps.

Giant pounding footsteps.

Coming closer.

And then they were there.

5

CHAPTER FIVE

"Hey man, is this the line for the lady?" A voice sounded behind us.

I'd like to say only the ghost screamed.

I'd like to say only the ghost jumped, bounced off the energy field and tried to keep from firing off a magic spell at the obvious human standing behind us, holding a guitar in both hands.

Let's just say I said it, okay?

Only the ghost was scared.

Not me.

Not for that.

"What the hell did you do?" Elvis screamed.

"I shot him," I stammered.

The ghost floated over to the prostate form on the ground and reached down to check his pulse. His fingers slipped through his neck and the body shivered.

"At least he's not dead."

"He snuck up on us," I argued.

"Look-"

A giant hand whistled out of the darkness and batted me eight rows out into the cotton field.

"Out!" Elvis shouted.

"Thanks for the warning," I rolled over and up.

A twelve foot tall Troll stood outside the energy field and stared at the unconscious man in the dirt. He lifted up a five foot long foot and prepared to squash him like a bug.

I winged a spell at his big toe, the zap lifted him up and knocked him back on his posterior with a puff of crunching dirt.

The Troll howled.

"You didn't tell me there was a Troll in my territory," I shouted as I shoved aside the cotton plants and made my way back toward the crossroads.

"I didn't know," Elvis floated to meet me halfway, the tether making his job of finding me easy.

"How do you not know a twelve foot creature is living around here?"

The Troll rolled over to his scabby knees and made its way to wobbly feet.

I grabbed the next in line guy and dragged him on the other side of the shield, trying to keep him out of harm's way.

The witch was inside the protective dome pointing and laughing.

I could see the other guy still curled around his guitar and crying.

Guess he didn't like the price he paid for greatness.

The Troll started stomping back toward the crossroad.

"How's she planning to give the magic to the Troll?" I circled around the dome and tried to think about taking it out.

They are nigh on impervious.

Magic affects them, but it has to be just right.

Just right everything.

Right spot, right spell, right time.

Trolls are magic creatures themselves, and normally belong on the other side of the veil. The Sidhe used them a lot in the War.

And abandoned them over here when they lost.

Most people think of Trolls as big dumb lumbering idiots.

Those people end up dead quick.

Trolls are smart, some of the smartest in Fae. They just look dumb. It's the size, and their faces, and the perpetual look of befuddlement that is their bone structure.

But they can outthink most humans on any given day, and the fact that this one was still around eighty years after the War ended meant he was as intelligent as they get.

One sign of intelligence was finding a partner.

Like a black magic woman stuck in a backwater community on the edge of the Mississippi.

I tried to think about a bridge close by.

One thing about Trolls is they have to have a bridge.

Over troubled water, over gorges, over canyon or dell. It's part of their make up, like a dragon drawn to greed.

Did the train rumble over a bridge while I was conversing with the vampire?

The Troll roared and rushed me.

"Eeep!" Elvis shrieked.

I wasn't too worried. Trolls are big and twelve feet tall was twice my height. It meant he could cover ground fast, but not as fast as a scared man can move.

I hightailed it back the other direction with a plan to rope a dope him until he was worn out, then maybe blast him in the eye with an icepick spell.

I did remember a bridge. A change in the rumble on the tracks. A large creek a mile or so away, over a creek or bayou.

It must have been his home.

I wondered how many runaways had disappeared around here. How many hobos riding the rails never made it through.

I should have been paying better attention.

Because I didn't hear the Troll running behind me.

By the time it registered, I smacked into a leg that felt like tree bark.

Smart Troll.

Stopped running and waited for me to make the circle.

Dumb Marshal. Should have kept my head in the game.

It reached down with massive fingers and grabbed one arm to lift me up. It grabbed a dangling leg in the other and held me parallel to the ground, started pulling like a kid with a wishbone.

It smiled, and drooled and I could see yellow eyes the same color as the witches as it pulled me up level with its nose to watch my final seconds.

6

CHAPTER SIX

People can't see ghosts.

Because most people don't have magic. Mediums can because that is their special power. Some witches can. Depends on the spell and their particular brand of magic faith.

As in, believe you can see a ghost strong enough, the power manifests like that.

Cats can see ghosts.

All cats.

Which is why they are magic.

And of course other magical creatures can see ghosts.

Like Trolls.

Elvis used the tether to catapult himself right into the Trolls face, a screaming banshee of physical ineffectiveness.

But the Troll didn't know that.

It let go of my arm to bat away the spirt wailing and whipping around its eyes, jabbing spiritual hands toward unprotected yellow eyes.

Then it dropped me.

Headfirst into the hard Mississippi dirt.

Lucky me, I rolled at the last minute and just did a backflop into the dust. Not even a cotton plant to break my fall.

Like landing on dirty concrete.

I lay there flopping for a second, trying to find the wind that was knocked out of me.

Then I heard the witch screaming.

The power of the soundproof energy dome was dissipating as she yelled at the Troll.

Something about "Get him!" or "Squish him!"

I didn't wait to find out which.

Even though I couldn't get up, I could wiggle my finger. It was enough to focus my mind and zap us away.

I'm not strong enough to go far.

The Judge can move us anywhere across the globe. My wife and her sister could move us a couple thousand miles.

I made it two hundred yards and poofed back into the dirt, still not breathing.

Elvis got dragged through the air by the tether, his scream making a doppler effect in the still night.

He was smart enough to shut up when he stopped, and floated in the dark above my head.

"You okay?" he whispered.

I moved my mouth like a fish, but no sound came out.

"I thought he was going to split you in half," said Elvis.

He folded his legs into a lotus yoga pose and sat in the air just over me. I didn't appreciate the view.

But I couldn't say anything until my diaphragm stopped

making spasms.

When it did, I rolled over and shoved myself to my knees to peer over the tops of the cotton plants.

"How long was I down?" It took a couple of breaths just to get the question out.

"Twenty minutes," he told me. "Not that ghosts can tell time. We don't need to, you know. Time for us is just a drop of forever."

"Don't get philosophical," I warned him.

That took a few more breaths.

The Troll and Witch must have thought we left.

They could have figured we were coming back, because she was in the middle of completing the ritual with the large creature, foregoing the second man still unconscious off to the side.

I might have hit him a little harder than I thought.

Blame the ghost. He's a squealer and the noise startled me.

"Gross," Elvis whispered next to my ear, sending a spark from the tip of my finger.

The light caught the eyes of the witch and the creature, but not enough to make them stop, just pause.

"Yep," I snapped.

I was getting tired of getting scared.

The ritual to steal lifeforce through sex magic was the same as to give it.

That's what made Elvis say gross.

Cause the Troll laid down on its back, and the witch went to work on getting him ready. It didn't take much, then she climbed on and straddled him.

It wasn't pretty, and the physics of it was all wrong. This time the witch was the one screaming.

"I just can't wrap my head around why?" Elvis turned away and floated his back to the sight. I turned to join him.

"Magic transfer," I said.

"But to what purpose? A witch and a troll can make magic together, but why? She's stealing essence, so that makes her live longer, otherwise I would think she would get life points in exchange for the sex magic," he said. "But we're missing something."

His face crinkled in concentration.

"Do we really need a why?" I asked.

"I need to understand what's going on."

I stood up in the darkness and adjusted everything that had shifted in my fall and escape, starting with my spine. It popped like it was protesting and I bit back a groan.

"I'm going to let you figure it out," I told him.

"I can't stay here while you go Marshalling," he pointed to the invisible line that tethered him to me.

"Then you'll have to think it up on the move," I told him. "She's doing black magic and I can't let that stand."

Plus I had a thing about Trolls.

I'd run into a platoon of them back in the Sidhe War.

They were vile creatures who belonged on the other side of the veil, and when you catch them munching on a battalion of allies in the woods of Bastogne, let's just say rage is a powerful magic multiplier.

I reached down and tapped into a little of that, then sprinted toward the duo doing it in the dirt.

They couldn't hear me over the screaming.

She was not enjoying herself.

The Troll turned his head toward me though. Maybe he felt me running, just as I felt his footsteps pounding toward the dome earlier.

He tried to move his hands and bat the witch away.

I didn't give him a chance.

I channeled a spell into one of his yellow eyes and blew out the back of his head in a spray of gore and guts that painted the Mississippi landscape like a Rorschach pattern.

The witch stopped screaming as something happened in the magic transfer.

She tried to hop off, hop down, hop away.

I quivered a spell into her heart and popped it in her chest before she could do any of it.

She collapsed in a mound on the ground next to the Troll.

"Marshal?"

I turned to look at the wide eyed ghost beside me.

He just pointed.

The problem with interrupting a ritual spell is the build up of magical energy. A ritual is about layering and building, combining forces until the right level is reached. Then all of that pent up energy is released, which makes the completion of the spell possible.

All of that energy was in a bond between the dead Troll and the dead witch, a short black ribbon of shimmering darkness that boiled and churned with tiny purple streaks of lightning.

"Crap," I sighed.

"This is gonna hurt," Elvis advised.

The magic exploded in a thunderclap and for the third time that night, I was flying through the air and anticipating another hard landing.

7

CHAPTER SEVEN

I didn't pass out, though it took several minutes to catch my breath again.

"Thirty two minutes," Elvis said as I crawled back to my knees and stood on shaky legs again.

Mississippi needed some rain to soften up that soil.

I looked back at the mess of the ritual site.

The Troll was in pieces scattered around the crossroads.

The witch was a stain on the dirt. The two men willing to sacrifice their lifeforce in exchange for talent, possible glory were gone, parts of their clothes and guitars fluttering in the wind.

"I hope I never have to see something like that again," I told the ghost and started walking toward the tracks.

At least I thought I did.

Elvis had to adjust my direction.

Twice.

Guess I landed harder than I thought.

The tracks were right where we left them. Not that I expected them to move or anything, but after I bounced my head off the dirt a couple of times, I was wondering if the tracks had moved or if there was more magic afoot.

The twin rails ran in a straight line through the black countryside, a wash of stars bright enough to make the sky glow, but cast little light on the ground.

I turned south, double checked with Elvis to make sure it was the correct direction then hoofed it.

The rail line ran across country highways and backroads farms every couple of miles. We approached the fifth or sixth one and saw a beat up pickup truck waiting next to the yellow and black RR crossing sign.

For a moment, I thought it was mind, and the Judge was making magic happen again.

"Marshal?" the voice called from behind the driver's seat.

I pulled up a spell and got ready to cast it. It never paid to let down your guard in the middle of the night in strange country where no one was supposed to know you were there.

"The Judge sent me."

I let the spell go.

Not my truck, but I had to admire the fellow for his chosen form of transport.

Almost anyone could say those words, but if they Judge didn't actually send the man behind the wheel and he said it, then hell could rain down on him.

Literally.

The Judge was that strong.

8

CHAPTER EIGHT

I opened the passenger door and slid into the worn seat. A handsome man with rugged Nordic features nodded as I buckled up, then dropped the truck in gear and rumbled across the tracks.

"Eric," he held out a hand.

I twisted to shake it, surprised when he moved his grip to my forearm and squeezed for three shakes.

It was an old-fashioned warrior handshake, and gave me a tingle of the magic coursing through his veins.

And something else.

A possession. The man had a spirit inside of him, not a demon, but a tag along, something he was born with.

He let go before I could get a full impression, but he smirked as he did so. The Viking knew what he intel he was sharing with the handshake.

"My Shield wall ran into a nest of biker vamps in Louisiana. I lost my Hund and had to go make a report to the Jarls."

"Jarl's?"

A word I hadn't heard in years, not since my time on the border in the Sidhe War.

"Earl's," he Americanized it for me. "Our wise leaders."

Someone could have hung a coat on the sharp way he said wise. Eric wasn't impressed with the Jarls, or one of them at least.

"One of them told me to be on that crossing at midnight and wait for you to show up."

He glanced over at me.

"They had the timing right."

"Biker vamps?" I tried to change the subject.

"My Jarl told me to tell you the Judge sent me. Who's that?"

I glared at the black sky through the open passenger window.

"No one of consequence."

"You're going to pay for that," said Elvis.

He sat on the seat between us, paying extra attention to keep his non-corporeal thigh from touching the driver, lest he shiver like a ghost ran across his grave.

Which pretty much put him in direct contact with me, making me shiver like a newborn in a snowstorm.

Eric reached up and turned the heat over all the way, then adjusted his vents so the blast turned away from him.

"What did you fight back there?"

He was a warrior.

I could tell by the scarred hands, the thick shoulders, the look in his eye. He was an apex predator, which I guess he would have to be if he was in charge of a Shield wall hunting Vampires.

"Troll."

He made a whistling noise with his lips and looked at me with newfound respect.

"Alone?"

I nodded.

"Damn."

He said it with respect, which made the aches and pains feel a slight bit better.

"I knew Marshals were tough, but a Troll alone. That just means you're crazy."

"A voo doo witch was trading lifeforce with it," I said.

"A witch and a Troll?" he scoffed. "You've moved past crazy and over into insane territory."

I could feel the respect seeping away.

"Borderline stupid."

I felt a surge of anger.

Who the hell was this guy, warrior or not. Damn Vikings and their messed up-

"I'm just messing with you," he smiled.

Guess he could tell I was pissed.

"And you shopped shivering. Took your mind off being cold, off the aftereffects of battle."

He did. I had.

"Been there," the Viking continued. "Done that. Burned the Tee Shirt."

"Trolls?"

"No, just vampires. The Trolls in Norway are twice as big as American Trolls. They trapped them in the Mountains with giant barriers disguised as power lines. Most of the ones left over here are runts."

I'd found the mountain Trolls in the woods. They were bigger.

Still, fighting a twelve foot runt wasn't anything to sneeze at.

And a witch, though she didn't do much fighting.

And didn't do much good for my hunt.

"You can sleep if you want," Eric offered. "I don't know what you're planning in the Big Easy, but something is going down."

"I met a vampire on the train," I told him. "A conclave."

His eyes flashed red in the darkness of the cab as the spirit inside him surged to the surface.

I watched him fight it back, an internal battle that only showed on his face, the grit of his teeth, the crinkled eyes.

"Did you kill it?" he growled.

Still fighting.

"Only allowed in self-defense," I told him and he nodded. "We talked."

"Talking doesn't do much good with the bloodsuckers," he said.

My turn to nod.

The Normanii were a group of vampire fighters dedicated to keeping the world safe from the undead. They had one reason for existence, to end the scourge of vampires.

They were pretty locked in on that worldview.

And they were damn good at their job.

But the Marshal's had to see things just a little different.

Shades of grey, I liked to call it on my ethical slide rule.

A lot of vamps could exist with humans, there were enough of the goth types that would offer up blood for the asking.

I could no more cast a vampire than I could a witch without reason.

The reason didn't have to be much, sure. It could be a perceived threat, or a hint of one.

But I tended to err on the side of basic decency, a live and let live policy that usually served me well.

Until I got my ass handed to me on a platter.

Then I could go crazy with the magic.

"Did he tell you what they were con-claving about?"

He played with the word, and I bet under different circum-stances we could be friends or drinking buddies.

If I was allowed to have either.

"Didn't get the chance," I told him. "Ran across a ritual at a crossroads before I could get more out of him."

The Viking nodded.

Then he gripped the wheel and glared at the road, the red glow in his eyes softening to just a circle around the iris that I could only see when he glanced over at me.

That was my cue to shut up and catch some shut eye, so I hunkered down against the door of the truck and tried to do just that.

Elvis was quiet enough to let me.

But sleep wouldn't come.

Instead I thought about my wife, and where she went missing. It was on a Troll hunt, a mission for the Judge.

No word on what happened.

No sign of where she went.

Like she just disappeared.

I bet he poofed her straight to the fight though. No messing around with bumming rides on trains and trucks trying to clean up a mess.

That was part of his way for punishing me, I bet.

And with that thought, I drifted down into a nap.

9

CHAPTER NINE

The Viking dropped me off on a corner where the trolley tracks crossed the road, just as he had picked me up near tracks a few hours earlier.

Dawn gathered on the horizon, ready to assault the morning and wash the city with daylight.

"I'll be seeing you," the Norseman promised as he rumbled away, and I gave him a small wave he could see in the rear view.

"Does she know you're coming?"

"Usually I'd tell you and you would do whatever it is that the Watcher's do to prepare the way."

"So, you didn't tell anyone?"

He hung there six inches off the ground with a very judgy look on his face.

I should know, I'd seen it on the Judge's often enough.

"I told you, didn't I?"

"I don't have access to the resources I once did."

"But you could put it out on the ghost network."

"I could," he agreed. "But this Watcher would have to know a ghost and talk to a ghost and so far as I can remember from the archives, this isn't normal."

He waggled one ghost finger between him and me.

"You're an Elvis impersonator, Elvis," I told him. "There's nothing normal about you."

"We could try calling."

"Does she own a cell phone?"

"Hannah?"

"That's who we're talking about."

"How would I know that?"

"Watcher Rolodex?"

He patted his pockets.

"Must have left mine in my other coat."

Smart. Ass. Ghosts.

"Can you find a ghost neighbor and do the network thing to get me to his house?"

"That? Sure, I can do that easy."

He floated to the end of the tether, which was about fifteen feet when he stretched out with his toes pointing back at me. I could see animated hand gestures at a patch of air that was completely blank.

For all I know, the ghost was making it up.

But after a moment, he came back with a smirk on his features.

"Follow me," he said in a very Lurch like voice.

At least he still had jokes.

"The game is afoot," I told Elvis as we started walking.

"You think you're going to Sherlock Holmes this?"

"No man, I think I'm walking."

It beat waiting for the trolley.

I wasn't sure what I could figure out anyway. The witches and the vampires making a move around the same time hinted at bigger forces involved.

Bigger forces made me think Sidhe.

And if the Sidhe were making a play to get back into the world, everybody was in a heap of trouble.

We beat them back in WW II when the Nazi's aligned with them in a domination attempt.

They almost established a foothold at Dresden Germany, but I was one of the wizards there that stopped them.

It destroyed the city.

The Allies took the brunt of the heat for the destruction, claiming it was a bombing that got out of hand.

I could see the Judge's hand in that.

No need to put the blame on the back of a young wizard just coming into his power.

And I'm not even a fire mage.

I just popped some magic into the wrong munitions bunker and then things got out of hand.

"You're shivering again," Elvis said and floated a little bit of distance between us. "Sorry."

"Wasn't you," I told him. "Just remembering."

"Wife? Witches?"

"War."

Elvis nodded.

"You were in it, right?"

Still guessing. It must have been the worst kind of torture for him, a man who relied so much on his mind and memory to suddenly start to lose access to it.

When we got to Hannah's, I'd put her to work on it too.

"So, where is she?" I asked the ghost after we had wandered around for a couple of hours.

"I think-" he started to say.

"Don't think," I snapped. "Know."

He had led us to three houses so far, each in opposite directions and far from where we were. I was hot, hungry, still sore from the previous night's activities.

Which would have been as fun as hell to say if I was with a lady, but I wasn't.

Or technically I was with a witch and a Troll, and they were doing it, but I was trying to stop it.

Not in a prudish sort of way, because hey, when in Rome, but we were in Mississippi not Italy.

I put a stop to it and paid a price.

The bill was coming due.

My head hurt. My feet ached. And I wanted food in my belly. Now.

We were on the fringe of the Ninth Ward, the district that suffered the most during the destruction of Hurricane Katrina. I was still passing scars from nature's battle, bald lots between refurbished houses, a few remnants of shattered homes still lingered, and an oasis on the boulevard.

A café.

Not the café that brought us here, but another, just a tiny little mom and pop grill, soda signs in the windows, four metal tables out front and what I'm sure heaven must smell like filtering through the smoke from a vent in the wall.

I made it to the table and sat to wait for service.

An elderly black man with white hair stuck his head out of the door and gave a friendly smile.

"You got to order in here," he said. "But I'll bring it out when you're done."

I shoved out of the chair and moved inside to the counter.

It was an old shotgun house, converted to commerce after the hurricane and serving up some fine cuisine to the locals.

One side was reserved for the grill and galley kitchen, six tables ran down the opposite wall. Everything scrubbed and polished and cared for.

My kind of place.

I studied the chalkboard menu and opted for a burger, loaded and an ice cold bottle of Turbodog.

"Go on out front," said Mr. Friendly.

I paid him with the black card

He twisted off the top to the beer and handed me a stack of napkins to carry out with me.

I sat in the mid-day sun and sipped my local beer, letting the brown ale bite a little from the cold. It felt good.

Normal.

Not at all like a man on a witch hunt.

Then he brought the burger.

Hand patted, hand sliced onions and tomatoes, butter bun made at a bakery across town. I scarfed down three bites and notices Elvis slobbering as he stared at me.

"Would you believe that's so good even I can smell it?" he leered at my sandwich.

I nodded and wiped the mayo mustard combo from the sides of my mouth.

Then the beer hit the taste remnants on my tongue and I moaned.

The ghost moaned with me.

I was really hungry or it was that good. I voted for the latter.

Hannah showed up ten minutes after I was done, a second beer in front of me, belly full and as content as a newborn sucking on a bottle.

I had even tipped triple on the second beer, just to piss off the Judge.

"I got a call to come pick you up," she settled into the seat across from me. "Why didn't you just come to my place?"

I pointed to the chair beside me.

"Someone couldn't remember your address."

Her eyes drifted over to the empty seat and back to mine.

"How many of those have you had? You're talking about yourself in third person."

"She can't see me," said Elvis.

"Can she hear you?"

"Are you drunk?" Hannah asked. "You're doing that talk to yourself thing now."

I grinned.

Nope, not drunk, not off two beers, but mellow for sure. Too tired to worry about it, the aches were disappearing as the food and alcohol worked their magic at the molecular level on my system.

"I've got a lot to tell you," I told her.

"And I've got a lot to tell you. There's something big going on," her brown eyes grew wider, either in excitement or fear.

Maybe a little of both.

I finished the bottle and let her lead us back to her place so we could talk in private.

10

CHAPTER TEN

Hannah had a shotgun style home between two empty lots. She did the rehab herself, down to the plumbing and electric, then put a fence around all three to create a hidden oasis off the road.

The yellow siding looked like a splash of Caribbean lemon against the cool blue metal roof.

A wide porch stretched across the front.

It looked over green sod and a ground deck that was almost as long as the house, extending three quarters of the way down one side.

A well-used firepit occupied the center of the deck and even from here, I could sense the wards and spells.

There were protection spells interwoven with the fence, and ritual carvings etched into the deck wood. More lines sparkled in my mage sight as I studied the spells, for safety and comfort, for peace and knowledge, for serenity.

"Smart, Elvis observed. "I bet this neighborhood has the lowest crime in the city."

"Try no crime," said Hannah.

"Doesn't that attract attention," we had to wait for her to invite us to slip past the wards.

"Are you kidding? The NOPD want to give me community leadership awards. I'm tempted to take them but no room on my shelves for baubles."

She led us into the door, past more wards that I felt pop over my skin as we pushed through, like walking under a layer of humidity. The living room had plank floors, plank shelves, a rock fireplace and books. Everywhere.

All the flat surfaces were covered with them. Paperbacks, hard backs, research tomes and pulp novels were stacked on the shelves, the table, even the arms of the long sofa.

"Been doing some research," she grinned and shoved some aside so I could sit.

She perched in the overstuffed leather chair angled on the fireplace and stared at me with glistening eyes, pert and alert.

"You heard about Elvis," I said.

It happened quick, but word travelled at the speed of light in our paranormal world. She nodded.

"Comes with the territory," she said. "He shouldn't have gone in the field with you."

"He didn't."

She didn't know the details.

"He was locked behind his wards at his home. The witches got in."

She sat a little straighter and didn't look nervous or scared, like I expected. She looked excited.

"You brought him here before," she said. "I just assumed he

got killed following you. You know, once more into the breech."

"I can think for myself," Elvis spat.

Hannah shivered.

"Are you cold?" She asked. "I can start a fire."

I shook my head. A fire and this sofa on a full belly would make me lazy. Add to that the fitful sleep in a truck and it was a recipe for a nap.

"They had power," I told her. "I don't know where it was coming from."

"The Leyline," Elvis said.

"It was more than that."

"More than what?" she asked.

"The Leyline."

She dug through a stack of books and pulled out a leather-bound volume she plopped into her lap.

"I'll get started on some research," she told me. "In the meantime, you look wiped. Why don't you kick back and get ready for tonight?"

"What's tonight?" My senses went on high alert.

I mean I knew what I had to do, what I was here to find, but I thought that might require a little old-fashioned foot work. The paranormal community in the Big Easy was spread out, with different communities operating on various levels.

And a vampire conclave.

But someone would have seen a zodiac demon roaming around.

It just might take a while to find it.

"I thought you knew," she chewed on a strand of dirty blond hair she tucked between her lips as one hand flipped through crisp pages.

"I got a message that you were going to a graveyard tonight

for a midnight meeting. Same time I got the word to pick you up.”

“No one told me.”

She shrugged her bony shoulders.

“Guess I was supposed to.”

She tucked the book in on her lap and buried her chin into it, eyes skimming as she searched for knowledge.

I searched the room to see if I could help, but decided everyone would be better served if I grabbed forty winks.

So, I lay back on the couch and don’t remember passing out.

11

CHAPTER ELEVEN

"Marshal?"

"Yeah Elvis?"

"Am I the only one who thinks meeting this person in a graveyard is creepy?"

"Nope. But this is a cemetery."

The ghost screwed up his face in concentration and tried to figure out the difference.

"You were the one to tell me," I reminded him.

That made it worse. His eyes squinted closed as he tried to force his mind to sift through whatever was going on up there and pull that memory to the front.

It made me feel sorry for him, but I couldn't say that, since that would make him feel worse.

Nobody wants to hurt a ghost's feelings.

Instead I looked away and tried to make it sound like I was

just thinking out loud.

"A graveyard is just where they put bodies. But a cemetery is a celebration of life. You told me I could tell by the monuments."

"And mausoleum's," he added.

"That's right."

"I remember," he said in a sigh. "I did tell you that."

"Since you told me, I figure this is a cemetery and not just a boneyard."

"I feel like there are ghosts all around us."

"Watching."

"Watching," agreed the Watcher.

"There are."

Elvis shivered.

"You're kidding me right?"

I shook my head and tipped the hat back. A Stetson would have been overkill, especially for that whole cowboy fetish the Marshal of the West and I had going.

So for me, it was a trucker cap from a small company in Arkansas that said Get After It.

I never asked what IT was, but it seemed like good advice, in a general sense.

"I don't know much about the ghost realm," I told him. "It's there, next to ours, the same but different."

"You just described every place in America," he hiccupped.

I almost asked him if he was hiding a flask, and if so, why was he hiding it when it would be much easier to share.

But we were on duty, and though magic marshaling duty was very different from normal law enforcement, it probably wouldn't look good to meet the woman we were supposed to meet with the smell of whiskey on my breath.

Unless she was into that sort of thing.

A shadow stepped out from behind one of the crumbling marble mausoleums.

Elvis chirped out a scream.

It made me jump and flick a finger in its general direction.

Sparks bounced off a protective shield and splattered into the black dirt of the cemetery.

"Stop," said a high pitched voice with a nasal quality. "That tickles."

And I was transported back.

A few years ago Elvis and I made the trip down here to help find a Watcher when the old one moved on.

Nothing nefarious about it, the guy was just old. He lived to eighty four and had a good life.

The Marshal of the West was on assignment and the Judge suggested the Memphis watcher and I make the trip.

We got into some trouble with a small medium at large, when a psychic Gnome masquerading as a fortune teller went up against the Dixie Mafia for something she saw in her crystal ball.

Like they say in the movies, it was the start of a friendship.

Nothing beautiful about it though for two reasons. First, we hardly spoke since then, because she was west of the river and it would better for her to work with the Marshal on this side of the muddy water.

Second she wasn't beautiful.

I'm not trying to be cruel. She may have been once.

There were even hints of it in her playful eyes. But now she was a mass of wrinkles and lines, gray hair like a helmet on her tiny head.

Knu barely topped four feet, all arms and elbows, knees and shins, with little meat to her torso.

And she was literally a Gnome, one of the ancient creatures of Fae, left here on earth and surviving alongside humanity. Often hidden. Or like this one, hidden in plain sight with a shop off the French Quarter and a steady stream of client's ready to part with silver in exchange for a glimpse of their future or lost loved ones.

"Sorry about that," I called out to the dark shadow next to the crumbling marble wall.

Katrina did a lot of damage to the cemeteries, and rehabilitation dollars were more focused on the living than the monuments to long dead men and women.

"The last man to pop off that fast was so glad to see me," she scrunched up her face in a smile showing still really strong white teeth. "What's your excuse."

"I'm glad to see you too," I sputtered.

I forget the medium could have a dirty mind.

"Alright, infant," she chided as she picked her way through the monuments and statues to where Elvis and I stood.

"I forgot just how prudish American minds can be when it comes to something so natural."

"I've heard your dirty talk," I reminded her. "Nothing natural about it."

She snickered into the back of her hand, then threw her arms around me for a long hug.

"I've seen you," Kun told me.

There was a whole world in those words and the sadness in her tone made me feel like sobbing.

Who knew comfort could come in fun size packages.

"Asshole," she batted my chest and stepped away.

"Stop reading my mind," I told her.

"Stop being so obvious."

She told me once that reading minds takes little effort, so some of her magic goes into blocking off almost all of it.

Touch made it harder to block, which is why she normally kept her distance.

"That's no pistol in my pocket," I winked to let her know I was glad to see her.

And I could be just as far in the gutter as any other Gnome. She cackled.

"I missed you Marshal," she said. "Who's your friend?"

She nodded over my shoulder.

"My Watcher."

"Taking his job a little too literally," she said in her accented voice.

She never told me where she was from, but Gnome meant old country, Germany or Ireland back before they were called Picts and Gaul's.

"He's tethered to me," I told her.

Her eyes grew wide in the dark.

"Tethered to a human? That's not possible."

I indicated the ghost hanging around over my shoulder.

"It's never happened," she muttered. "Did you tell your Judge about this."

I nodded.

"And he didn't say anything, did he?"

I shook my head.

No need to talk if she can read my mind.

"Just like him," she cursed under her breath. "Arrogant son of a-,"

"Whoa," Elvis interrupted before she could call down the wrath of a man more powerful than some gods on all of us. "What do you mean never happened before?"

Her long fingers seemed an odd fit for her tiny body. That didn't stop her from pointing one at me.

"He shouldn't be strong enough for you to do it."

"But I picked him," Elvis answered. "Well not really picked. I was thinking of him when the witches got me. And abracadabra."

She nodded, a thoughtful look on her wrinkled face.

"Nope, still shouldn't do it."

"A death curse?"

"From a Watcher?" she dismissed it with a sniff. "It's a mystery Marshal, I'll give you points for bringing me something fun to ponder."

"You didn't see it in my future?"

Her eyes grew cloudy and sad, and she blinked something out of them before her face took on a grim set.

"It's something for me to think on while you get to work on the work that you do."

"Thank you for the clarity," I said.

"Follow me," she curled up a finger and pushed past me.

Like I had a choice.

I followed her diminutive shadow through the cemetery to a wrought iron fence that bordered a greenspace full of cypress trees that ran along a creek behind the wall.

"I didn't know there were woods in the City," I said in wonder.

She responded by touching my chin and pulling my face to look at her.

"Sshh."

I nodded. She pointed that long finger again.

And I could see through the woods to a clearing. Not too far away, just a couple of hundred yards at most.

Another alter.

Another ritual.

This one a couple hundred years old instead of a couple of thousand.

"Break it up," said the Gnome.

She pressed a business card into my palm and stepped back into the darkness, so that all I could see were her overlarge eyes, glowing with a soft tint in the blackness.

"Find me when you're done," she said.

And disappeared.

"You know what that is?" Elvis asked from next to my ear.

I tried not to jump.

Mostly succeeded.

"I smell T–R–O–U–B–L–E," I whispered.

"Those are witches Marshal," said the ghost. "I think we are F–U–C–"

12

CHAPTER TWELVE

A local coven was holding a shotgun wedding.

"Is this a case of wife or death?" Elvis whispered from my shoulder.

I snickered, which drew all the eyes in the clearing toward me.

Even the groom.

Wide brown cow eyes the size of cheese Danish, eyebrows practically touching the widow's peak of his hairline.

Not in a surprised way, but in a "please rescue me and I'll be your man-servant forever way."

He looked rough.

Ever heard the expression ridden hard and put up wet? He looked like twice that.

Big black circles under his eyes, pale complexion and thin wane lips compressed into a tight line as if he was holding back a scream.

"Spell bound," Elvis said.

That would explain the lips.

"Excuse me ladies, while I whip this out," I quoted my favorite line that drew a ton of laughs each time I said it as I shifted open my leather bomber.

The light from a disco ball sparkled off the silver star badge on my belt with the words MARSHAL magically enhanced so that all in the room could see.

No one laughed at my joke though.

There were a lot of glares.

Some minor hissing, like cats that get scared before they skedaddle.

"Tough crowd," I told Elvis.

"You get no respect."

I stepped into the clearing and moved to the edge of a salt circle.

"Ladies," I cleared my throat. "Wanna tell me why you've got a magical barrier around your special day?"

"You're not welcome here."

This from the wiccan looking one on the alter. She was a bouncy ball of rotund energy, practically vibrating from the magic she was pulling from the earth.

Whatever they had planned, I felt sorry for the groom.

"Welcome or not, I'm here to stop what you're doing."

The shotguns I mentioned?

They were literal.

While the salt circle was designed to contain the magic within, and I couldn't shoot a spell through the shimmering wall of glowing green, the witches must have pulled a reverse on it.

Which meant they could shoot out.

Shotguns.

Literally.

I watched three of them swing up from muscular WWE looking witches where the bridesmaids would have stood in a traditional wedding.

I flicked a shield spell up with a twitch of my fingers, almost like a soft snap and three rounds of birdshot bounced off like hurricane rain on a tin roof.

They were double barrels of fun stuff so I waited for the second blasts to echo through the clearing, then scooted a little closer to the salt line.

A quick swipe of my toe would disrupt the circle and give me access to sling a few spells into the group.

I didn't count on the familiars.

Some people have guard dogs, this coven had guard cats.

Enormous Maine Coon Cats, which made Rottweilers shiver in their chains.

One for each witch, which meant thirteen descendants of an amorous union of saber tooth tigers with woolly mammoths launched at me all at once.

I caught movement from the corner of one eye, saw a shadow in the corner of the other and did the only thing a human can do in a spot like that.

I ducked.

Two massive bodies slammed into each other with a roaring meow, and landed on top of my head just as a couple more two hundred pounds of cat flesh slammed into me.

We all tumbled across the clearing in a hissing, spitting, screaming jumble of limbs, claws and biting.

Mostly by me.

I had one cat by the tail when we stopped and came up

swinging like a Olympian in a hammer throw event. It yowled as it plowed into the other cats when they came in swiping, eight inch claws dashing for my face.

The swing bought me time, at least a foot of breathing room and that was all I needed.

Marshals are like gunslingers of the old wild West, except where those folks used six guns, we used magic.

Thought made real.

Each magic user is unique in their ability. Some need time to cast a spell, construct the thought, bind the elements and send it forth into the world.

Others need to gather ingredients for potions and boil up some trouble.

I was a trained BattleMage, and the Judge instilled in us a discipline like no other on this planet.

We trained until our spells were ingrained so deeply, they were cast and complete before the thought was from one side of the brain to the fingers.

Magic at the speed of a synapse.

That meant the coven was in trouble.

Because they gave me time.

I snapped and froze the cats.

I snapped and melted the earth under a two foot section of the salt circle so it collapsed with a psychic plop.

I snapped and the witches were paralyzed where they stood.

And I was ready for anything else they might have planned.

Witches were notorious for booby traps and backups.

But the woods were quiet.

I sauntered up to the wedding alter, which was made up like a lace covered twin bed and noticed the trenches in the wood, stained with blood from previous weddings.

The groom was in for the night of his life.

The last one.

They were going to steal his life essence and sacrifice him.

"I bet you're glad I got here buddy."

His eyes screamed, but his mouth stayed shut tight.

"You ladies are coming with me," I prepared the spell to transport us all in front of the Judge.

"Marshal!" Elvis screamed.

It was a psychic scream, since he was a ghost and the only way you can hear a ghost is through your mind, not your ears.

Psychic screams were a migraine whammy that felt like someone took a baseball bat, jammed a bunch of ice picks through it, named it something sweet and innocent like Lucille and slammed it into your mind hole.

Hurt is an understatement.

Still I'm no geek off the street.

The Marshal is a world class magical bad ass, the toughest of the Battle Mage's, a true survivor. In a job where a lifespan is roughly eighteen months, I'd been doing it for a decade.

That's because some of my magic is pre-cog, which lets me see one second or two into the future.

Normally.

A vision that serves me really well unless I get a warning from my ghost partner that hits like a roundhouse from Ali after a rope a dope.

I thought I saw a shadow getting bigger.

Then it hit me.

13

CHAPTER THIRTEEN

Now I don't know where the Coven got a sabre tooth tiger from and truth be told I didn't give a damn.

At least that's what I wanted to think as it gripped my battered leather bomber in the two teeth that was its namesake and shook me like a tiny little mouse.

I thought the Maine Coon Cats were big.

They looked little puppies compared to the extinct tiger.

Or kittens I guess I should say.

Getting swung around like a felt toy made the old brain pan mix up electrical signals.

Elvis was trying to help.

Though tied to me by a tether, it wasn't physical so he wasn't flopping.

He was popping though, doing a little dance on the massive kitty head, or dry humping it, I couldn't be sure.

Either or the extinct cat was not impressed.

It dropped me from its jaws and swatted me like a ball of yarn through the air.

I smacked into a tree, crashed through some branches and landed sort of sideways at the base of the trunk.

I had just enough time to see the sabre tooth bounding across the clearing to get me and raise my hand.

No claws.

The cat could have shredded me in one eviscerating swipe.

But it didn't.

It could have punched through my tender head with twelve-inch teeth.

But it didn't.

The damn cat looked like it was smiling.

I held back and regretted it cause the super-sized kitty popped me up in the air with a twist and sent me sailing again.

"Don't hurt Harold," someone called out.

I plopped down and wondered who the hell was Harold.

Then the defense took the field.

I wish I could tell you it was glorious. That the witches trembled in fear and there was lots of cowering.

There was.

Of me under a shield as kitty tried to get to its new toy.

I froze everyone and everything again and crawled out of my protective half dome like a turtle out of a shell.

Elvis floated down as I stood up.

"Thanks for the help," I groaned and meant it.

"Would you look at the size of that thing."

I felt it.

"They're extinct," he spun around and stared at me.

"That you remember," I stretched and listened to cracks,

pops and crackles as stuff inside me fell back in place.

"Laser tooth Tigers and cavemen, right?"

"Close," I told him.

"Yeah that didn't sound right."

He studied the massive frozen beast in front of us, focused on the sharp pointy teeth.

"Sword tooth? Knife tooth?" He guessed then grinned in victory as he snapped his ghost fingers.

They didn't make a sound.

"Razor tooth."

I nodded.

"You got it dude."

The ghost puffed up, confident in the win over his failing memory. Who was I to take it from him.

The bride and groom were stuck on the alter, the Coven leader in front of them.

I walked up, waved my hand around his head and thought release.

He staggered and stared in wide eyed wonder at the frozen tableau around him

"This your plan?" I asked.

"Not my plan, no."

His voice had a Cajun accent and a hint of something else. North maybe.

"You want it to happen?"

I kept one eye on the cats. Familiars are magical too and sometimes stronger than the witch or warlock they partner with. If one of them got loose, it could hurt.

"Not like this," the groom stuttered.

"Then go," I told him.

He was off like a sprinter at the Olympics and leaped the fence back into the cemetery.

"You know what's happening here?" I asked my ghost and realized with a start that he was sort of my familiar now.

I would have liked a bad ass Saber tooth tiger or a grizzly bear, but when life gives you melons you might be dyslexic.

"It's a ritual," he answered.

"I got that," I said wishing for my giant spirit animals. "What kind?"

He shrugged.

"A union."

"It is a wedding"

"Yes," he explained and for a moment there was the hint of my watcher there. "A union of power. These symbols are a trade, protection for power and the protection of power. This Coven has a weakness and it looks like the guy you let go was their key out of it."

Crap.

Was he a warlock?

"No," shrieked the witch behind me. "You ruined every-thing!"

And pop, just like that she broke my spell and let loose the cats of war.

14

CHAPTER FOURTEEN

Harold the Saber tooth was smarter than his partner.

As soon as the unfreezing thawed him out, he took two large leaps, knocked me down and covered me with his massive form.

The other cats bounced off his magical hide and plopped on their feet.

Waiting.

Harold bared his teeth, leaned in and licked me with his sandpaper tongue.

"Gross," I said. Cat kisses.

"I think he likes you," Elvis sang. "You ain't nothing but a cat though, licking all the time."

"Save it for karaoke," I pushed the cat back and sat up.

He inserted his head under my hand and allowed me to scratch him.

"Did you call him Harold?"

The Coven Leader stepped forward and tried to keep my attention.

"I am Beth," she introduced herself. "We are unfamiliar with you as the Marshal. We overreacted."

"Beth I hear you calling, but I can't come home right now," Elvis crooned.

"Wrong band," I stood up.

"What?" The witch and the ghost said at the same time.

He must have lost some memories of the Kings songs and was mixing them up with Kiss. The mind works in weird ways, just electrical impulses really, and when the wires get crossed or you go ghost, I guessed we were in uncharted waters.

"Nothing," I told her.

The rest of her Coven drifted in even lines behind her, six on each side, prepared to offer power if she needed it.

The shotguns were still pointed in my general direction though.

"I'm the Marshal of the East," I pulled aside the jacket to show the badge again. "And you should answer to the shield, not to the man."

She nodded and chewed on pouty lips.

Beth was a knockout in a girl next door way. Brunette hair pulled back in loose waves, beautiful face and not that I noticed, a really nice body under the flowing white gown. No bra.

"You're right," she agreed. "We're sorry. Things have been somewhat strained since the Marshal left town."

Left?

I kept that to myself. I guess I was expecting some back up, or at least a run in to let him know I was operating West of the river.

"But him being out of town shouldn't be that surprising," I

told her. "He covers all of the territory on this side."

She nodded in a way that was cute and demure at the same time and I sent out feelers to see if she was trying a spell on me.

Turned out no.

Turned out she was just a natural looker.

"He has been gone for some time," she said. "Long enough that others are starting to explore inroads into our fair city. You interrupted an alliance that would have saved a good many people."

"That's something for the Marshal to handle," I said.

"But he is not."

She watched me with golden brown eyes that shimmered in the flickering candlelight, waiting to see how I would react.

My partner, the one from the West was a hothead. A reputation for flying off the handle at the slightest provocations and using a hammer response when a scalpel was needed.

He would have blasted the witch, maybe all of them.

Some might not have survived.

It was in our right to do so because we chased, fought and captured the worst in the world.

Black magic is no joke.

But witches making an alliance was not a kill worthy offense.

Barely deserved a second glance from a Marshal of Magic, unless this union had disastrous consequences downstream.

And to find that answer, I'd need to visit the Gnome.

15

CHAPTER FIFTEEN

Harold let me go after a few more head scratches. He dismissed me in that feline way of turning up his nose and turning his back on me.

The Coven didn't though.

They watched me walk away, eyes tracking every step as if they expected me to turn and blast them at any moment.

I kind of liked the look of surprise on their faces when I didn't.

Elvis tagged along, but kept quiet.

I think he realized the mix up was a mess up, or he was trying to do a multiplication table. Something kept him occupied as we marched toward the fringe of the French Quarter and the little Shop of predictions therein.

The Gnome's home hadn't changed since our last visit. Maybe a few different veils on the wall and new candles added to the sconces, but it had a sense of eternal familiarity.

The crystal ball was in the same spot on the same stand, the chairs around the plush cushion top table a little more worn and faded

But the same.

She sat waiting in expectation as I pushed through the door.

"Did you figure it out?"

I shook my head.

"Not the witches I want."

"I know," she said. "But another problem to be dealt with."

"Not mine," I said.

Her keen eyes studied me as she crunched her caterpillar eyebrows together.

"He has not told you?"

"He who told me what?"

"Damn him to hell if he wasn't already cursed," her accent made the words sound elegant.

"Are we talking about the guy who ran away? He just told me it wasn't his plan," I explained.

She waved away the thought of him like an annoying gnat on a summertime eve.

"Digby Richmond," she sneered. "Mafia son is no matter to the things we are to discuss."

"Then I don't know who you're talking about."

She took a deep breath and said it slow, like she was explaining it to a child.

Which I suppose she was, at least to her. I was ninety something and didn't look it. She had been around a lot longer, but never gave me anything exact.

Gnomes were Sidhe and practically immortal beyond the veil. Here they could be different though.

I just didn't know how much.

"The Judge failed to tell you the Marshal of the West has fallen, a victim of one of the monsters you created."

I felt like a horse kicked me in the chest, then stomped my jibbly bits for good measure.

"Fallen?" I asked.

She could mean coma, or broken ankle. Heck, he could be down a well waiting on Tommie to show up with a posse and a rope to rescue him. Or turned warlock.

That thought sent a shiver up my spine.

She reached under the table and set a Stetson on it.

The brim was crusty with dust and blood, the shape a little ragged.

"No well, huh?"

She shook her tiny head.

"I do not know why he wouldn't share it with you."

I did.

Magic is about faith. And confidence.

And if a guy you thought was way tougher than you was taken out by a demon witch monster you set on the loose, it could shake the foundation of that confidence. A crack in the faith armor.

Doubt like that could be deadly.

It could affect the spell, the casting and the person behind it.

The answer was simple.

16

CHAPTER SIXTEEN

We returned to Hannah's place if not quite conquering victors, then at least a small tick in the W column. A win for the home team.

She didn't let the feeling last two steps past the door.

"I've got news," she stated.

Her voice was flat, her expression neutral.

I guess what she found out wasn't good.

"Those symbols you described for the ritual. They're a protection spell."

"I told you. A Union protection," Elvis snorted.

"A union protection spell," said Hannah.

I waved off the ghost so she could finish.

"Is it a gnat?" she asked. "I hate gnats. They get in all the time."

She glanced around for the flying phantom menace until I

could redirect her back to the thought on track.

"A Union protection spell?"

"The Coven you met is the weakest in New Orleans. Their Leader has only been in charge for a short while, less than a year. But her heart's in the right place."

"Nothing I enjoy more than an anatomically correct good witch."

"Right," Hannah rolled her eyes. "And Eww."

"It's the Big Easy, right. Got to let your freak flag fly."

"Keep it at half mast, okay? Her Coven made some enemies in the past few months."

"How?"

Hannah shrugged.

"I don't know."

"It's the question behind the question that is sometimes important," I told her. Let her hang that with my freak flag. I'm like a mullet, business up front, but party in the back.

"I'll find out," she answered and moved on.

"They made an enemy of a Voo Doo witch named Phyllis and now they're trying to partner with Dixie mafia for protection."

"You found all of that out in one night?"

"I've been watching," she smiled. "Sort of in the job description."

"Where is she?"

The smile fell away.

"I haven't found her yet."

"One more thing to work on."

She nodded and I pulled the Stetson from under my coat, placed it on the coffee table. Hannah took a long look at it and burst into tears.

"No," she repeated several times.

We watched her walk over to the leather chair and collapse into it, tuck her legs to her chest and bury her face in her arms. Sobs racked her body.

I glanced at the ghost, who shrugged his wispy shoulders.

"Would you react like that if I died?" I asked him.

"No," Hannah sobbed. "I barely know you. We've met twice. I'm sorry."

Her shoulders heaved.

"It's just not a nice way to find out your lover is dead."

"Well love me tender," Elvis crooned.

"Lover? He was your boyfriend."

She swiped the back of her hand across the tip of her nose to catch whatever might be clinging there and pawed at her swollen eyes.

"Lover," she corrected me. "Two consenting adults who agree to a physical relationship. You wouldn't understand."

She said the last part with a sneer that kind of hurt my feelings.

Did she think I was an old man?

Or was it a NOLA culture thing, a French influence lingering in the swampy air.

I let her cry as we watched, and after a few moments of the sounds of her sobs filling the air, they dried up.

Hannah excused herself to the bathroom, blew her nose and came back a little more composed.

She shifted a book to one side, picked up a notebook with a pen attached and began scribbling.

"I assume his affairs were in order."

I shrugged.

"Are yours?"

I nodded.

"Then we can assume his were as well. You are in the same line of work. Were," she sniffled and fought back a fresh round of tears.

"Do you have a replacement in mind?"

"I just found out tonight, but our employer might. Expect him or her to knock on your door."

"When?"

"I don't know."

"Are you the only Marshal in the States right now?"

"I don't know."

"Who's watching out for the paranormal community while you're off on this witch hunt?"

"I don't know."

"What the hell do you know Marshal!" she snapped, then the tears were back.

It made me wish someone would cry like that over me when I was gone. Maybe my wife would, if she could sense it wherever she was in the cosmos.

"Help her," Elvis said.

"How?" I mouthed so she wouldn't overhear me.

"Give her your shoulder."

"Huh?" again mouthing.

"A shoulder to cry on."

I nodded.

"Okay."

"What?" Hannah looked up through tears as I approached.

"I was just saying okay," I wrapped my arms around her and pulled her in for a hug. "There there, it's going to be okay."

"What are you doing?"

"Letting you cry," I told her.

She tried to push back, and when I turned loose, she gripped me by the lapels of my jacket and jerked herself back into my chest.

She buried her face against my shirt and started crying more.

Youth.

She was in her mid-twenties, close to the age of my now expired counterpart. Both of them reasonably good looking. Both of them fit, and young, and given how much time they spent together, it really wasn't a surprise it turned physical.

Like me, he'd probably pulled a night or two on the couch and perhaps one fire, one bottle of wine, one case to research had turned them onto and into each other.

She leaked her grief into my shirt, tiny shoulders quivering under my hands.

And I did what Elvis told me to do.

I let her cry on my shoulder and I kept my mouth shut.

17

CHAPTER SEVENTEEN

She wasn't quite cried out, but composed might be a better word for it. That's the way grief works sometimes. Go through a tearful jag and end up at a place where work is the focus.

I had no doubt there would be more tears, but an hour and a beer later, we were back on the streets hunting for a voo doo woman.

Hannah drove.

She had a blue VW bug with a green passenger door from a prior accident she refused to fix on principle, she told me.

The car puttered up and down the streets of the French Quarter as she searched for free street parking, and a space opened up two blocks from where she said we needed to go.

It was a nice evening for a walk. The sun was setting, the twilight time one of my favorites. It was happy hour, which didn't seem to matter much in the tourist traps that dotted the French Quarter. Every hour there was happy hour and the libations flowed freely.

Hannah fell in step beside me as we made our way to a small Voo Doo shop that occupied the front of a craftsman style home that looked like it had been there for a couple hundred years.

It had.

A plaque on the brick column that held one side of the metal gate said, "Built in 1846."

That was a lot of surviving to do for a simple wood structure with a recessed porch and lead pane windows. A thousand footsteps had worn the stone walk to a polished sheen, testament to her effectiveness and power, or the power of her marketing that made people believe.

A different kind of faith magic, but given almost two hundred years, enough time for it to start working.

Add to that some real mojo and the voo doo could be the hoo doo she do so well.

We watched a woman scurry past us clutching a red bottle to her ample chest. She refused to make eye contact.

"Love potion," said Elvis.

"Number Nine," Hannah spoke in my other ear.

Guess it was a Watcher thing.

We opened the door and wood chimes announced us with a clickety clack instead of gongs.

A young black woman with a tight afro stood behind the desk and smiled in greeting. She had a flowing peasant dress, and a red bandana around her neck, along with leather thongs, and some brass figurines.

"Welcome," she purred in a coffee rich voice. "What can I help you find today."

"I'm looking for Phyllis," I answered with a smile of my own.

Hers vanished.

Faster than any magic could make it.

"What do you want with her?" The eyes were guarded now, not so welcoming as a second before.

It is easy to tell if someone is a user and in the community.

All I have to do is show the badge.

If they are a normal person acting as clerk, they look at it and wonder why the ATF or DEA happens to be about. That's the letters a non-magical person would see etched in the infused metal.

A user though would see exactly what it is.

MARSHAL

And they would know.

Cause if the Marshal showed up at your door, chances are you were up to no good, starting to make trouble in your neighborhood.

The woman behind the counter glanced at the badge and froze.

"Don't shoot," she whispered, eyes ratcheting up to the size of small saucers.

"Don't make me," I growled.

I'll admit, the trucker's cap, though battered and worn, did not have the same menacing effect as my now deceased partner's Stetson. Didn't stop me from trying though.

I tilted up the brim and leaned over the counter on my elbows, finger pointed in her direction.

No need to tell her it was just for show, and overkill, I could do what needed to be done with just my mind.

"You Phyllis?"

"No," said Hannah and pointed to a picture on one of the shelves when I glanced over my shoulder.

The young woman in front of me was wearing a white softball tee shirt with red letters that said DEE on the front, next to an older elegant looking lady in the same kind of shirt, PHYLLISS on hers.

"She's making you look bad," said Elvis.

"Not quite," I said and stood up.

"Not quite what?" Hannah asked.

I'd talk to her about impressions and appearances as soon as we left the place. Aura is sometimes all about timing and keeping your mouth shut.

"She's not here!" Dee blurted out. "I don't know where she is."

The last part was a little too fast, a little too forced.

I hooked a thumb in my belt and shook out my index finger so she could see.

"You sure Dee?"

She gulped.

I watched her swallow.

"I'm sure."

Elvis floated on his tether and stuck his head through the wall. He pulled it through and blew away an imaginary dust ball.

"All dark in the back. Feels empty," he said.

"I think she's telling the truth," Hannah said, watching me instead of Dee.

We were really going to have to work on our good cop, bad cop routine.

But I felt that way too.

Dee was scared, but I couldn't say if she was more afraid of us or the voo doo woman we were hunting.

"Do you know when she'll be back?" I tried another track.

Dee shook her head, wide eyes dancing from me to Hannah

and back again.

"Let's go," I turned and started for the door.

"That's it?" Hannah trailed me.

"No, you're right," I turned from halfway across the room. "Dee, you know who I am, right?"

She nodded, a terrified look on her face. She didn't know me, but she knew what I was, and the reputation that the Marshal of the West left didn't taste good in most magic users' mouth.

"You know what Phyllis is, right?"

Another nod. More wide eyes.

"Then why isn't this place warded?"

I hadn't felt a single tingle stepping through, not even the residual magic of a homeward, the build up of energy people give off just living in a place.

"It's not her home," Dee said. "Just a shop, just for tourists."

"Then where is home?"

"I don't know."

I watched her eyes, watched the skin around her brow for any ticks, a trace of betrayal. But nothing moved.

Dee held my gaze and cringed like the lack of an answer was a crime in itself.

"No magic in here?" I asked.

She shook her head.

"Tell her I'll be back."

Dee nodded.

I led Hannah and Elvis back down the walkway.

"Where now?" she asked.

"A little less conversation, a little more action," the ghost of Elvis said.

I glanced over my shoulder and saw him staring at a spot on the sidewalk.

Three men waited.

Correction. Two half Trolls and the guy from the alter waited.

I bit back the urge to start slinging and instead pulled Hannah a little behind me so I could block her.

"Marshal," the man named Digby smiled. "No need for violence."

He stepped out of the shadows and under a street light, followed by the two boulders on either shoulder, and I could see he meant it.

His bodyguards weren't Trolls, just looked that way.

He saw me appraise them.

"You like? I picked them up on special when the Saint's went marching home," he beamed.

"Impressive."

"Bum knees," he added in an exaggerated whisper.

He held out a hand and I shook it.

"I wanted to say thank you for the thing you did," he glanced at Hannah.

"She knows."

"She does? Good, I don't have to hunt for the words. Discretion and valor, you know."

I doubted the son of a dixie mafia boss knew much about valor, but I wasn't going to be the first one to sling insults. The two goons orbiting him were armed, and if they started shooting, innocent people might get hurt.

"I didn't know there was so much magic in the world," Digby kept smiling. "But man, once you know where to look."

He pointed to the building we just abandoned.

"That place? Tourist trash. But the woman who owns it? Powerful magic."

He swung his hand up and down and whistled.

I didn't ask how he found me.

If he knew about magic, and he was connected, finding a Marshal who wasn't hiding would be easy.

But I did wonder what he was up to.

"You're welcome," I told him.

"I want to help you out," said Digby. "I mean, I would have married Angie in a heartbeat, for all the right reasons, but last night was not right."

I wondered if I should have him explain. Then I figured just to keep my trap shut. Digby struck me as the type of fellow who liked a good monologue.

His two bodyguards rolled their eyes.

Apparently, they had heard more than one before.

"I don't know why you're here," he said. "But you're not the normal Marshal for New Orleans."

"He's out of town," I told him.

Hannah sniffled.

"And trouble is brewing," Digby nodded. "I could tell that when they forced me into that ceremony last night. What kind of trouble."

I looked him up and down for a second.

"The magical kind, right? He grinned. "I'm not magic, no sir. But I've got some feelers out in this town. You could say, I know people who know people. And I pay my debts. My dad makes sure of it."

"Did your dad send you to find me?"

The two bodyguard nodded like they were in sync, heads bobbing up and down twice in slow motion.

Maybe they were more baby sitters than bodyguards.

"Ignore those guys," said Digby. "I told Daddy I wanted to thank you and he suggested I go look."

"You're welcome," I told him. "I was just doing my job."

"I know, but it's hard to not take it personally when someone saves your life."

"I don't think they would have killed you?" I shot a look at Elvis.

The ghost shrugged, eyes telling me he couldn't remember.

Lucky for me, he was hovering by Hannah, who thought my look was meant for her, and she shook her head no.

"The rituals weren't set up for blood."

That got Digby's attention.

He zeroed in on her, and I got a glimpse of the predator he could be. Not there, not yet, but if he followed in his Daddy's footsteps, someone he might become.

He looked at her like a hawk eyeing a field mouse.

"So much knowledge in a tiny package," he reached a hand around me to grip hers. "Digby Richmond."

"Hannah," she said.

His smile was charming her as he pumped her hand twice and let go, fingertips trailing along hers.

"Glad to meet someone else in the know, Hannah. Maybe one day soon we can trade stories and share what we learn."

"She knows just enough to get her in trouble," I said, trying to head off her blush.

"Excellent," Digby clapped. "Just like me. Just enough to stay in trouble, and thanks to you Marshal, still alive to keep finding it."

He winked at Hannah.

"But I'm staying out of it tonight."

He held up both hands to show they were empty.

"I'm just a messenger right now, and I want to tell you where you can find the purveyor of that establishment."

"That's a good deduction," I told him. "To think I'm looking for her."

"I didn't know, really," the smile again.

Either he was really innocent or really good at acting like it.

"I'm just connecting dots. You busted up a Coven ceremony. You go into their enemy's headquarters. I know you don't work for the voo doo woman, so I'm just assuming you're looking for her. Am I right? I'm right, aren't I?"

I gave him a nod. No harm. No foul.

"And I so happen to know where she is because some of my contacts stumbled across her in the hunt for you."

"Hunt?"

"Search," he backed up a step.

Guess I needed to dial down the paranoia a notch.

"She's at the St. Louis Cemetery," said Digby. "I hope that helps."

I looked at Hannah and she nodded.

"We can walk from here."

"I can offer a ride," said Digby.

He elbowed one of the guards in the ribs to use a wrist microphone to call up a big limo. Not a stretch limo, but a jacked up SUV large enough for a dozen people.

"We'll walk," I told the Dixie prince. "But I appreciate the offer. And thanks for your help."

"No problem Marshal," Digby climbed up into the back of the SUV. "Like I said, I always pay my debts. And you'll always have a friend in NOLA when you need me."

He shut the door before I could refuse such a kind offer, and we watched the Limo drive off.

"Which way?"

She pointed.

"It would have been faster to ride," said Hannah.

I took off marching toward the direction she indicated.

"We needed the time."

"We would have more time there if we drove," she huffed to keep up.

"We need more time to prepare," I answered. "Dee would have called to warn her we were looking."

"I would have liked to ride in the Limo," Elvis said as he floated along. "I haven't been in one of those since my prom."

18

CHAPTER EIGHTEEN

Remember when I told you about the whole faith magic thing? Belief is inherent in the workings of magic. If you don't believe, it won't work. Haitians believed in zombies. Not the shuffling "I'm hungry for brains," zombies, but Hattian Zombies. Come back from the dead, impossible to kill. A whole lot in common with golems from the Jewish tradition, not that weird voice guy from the Tolkien books.

I hate zombies.

New Orleans was a refuge for Haitians, especially after the devastating earthquake there in 2008. Hurricane Katrina did little to slow the immigration of the Hattian community to a town that embraced their traditions and witchcraft with a level of acceptance unseen anywhere in the U.S. There were several hundred thousand Haitians living in NOLA.

Which meant there was a lot of belief rolling around in the

air.

Belief a good wicked witch could pull on to enhance her magic. Not to mention tens of thousands of dead Haitians who while alive, believed.

"Hannah," I gulped.

We were staring at two dozen Haitian zombies spread out across the road.

She squeaked. I took that to mean, "What?"

"You have to get me to the Haitian cemetery."

"Squeak."

I translated that to mean, "Can you get us past the Haitian zombies blocking our path and closing in on us?"

"I'm going to take out this group," I told her. "But I need to get to the main cemetery and lock it down or they're just going to keep coming."

"Squeak." Or yes.

At least that's what I think she said. I'm a little rusty on my terrified noise translation. I have trouble enough keeping my own in.

Zombies are slow. They have one advantage and that is in overwhelming numbers.

If they catch you, they rip you apart. No eating brains, no coming back to life as a zombie if they bite you, at least no reported cases of it yet.

Zombies would grab you and tear your limbs off and you would bleed to death. They probably ate you, but I hadn't seen zombie work since the Elf Front in Germany.

The Sidhe's used zombies for a couple of battles. Those weren't Haitian zombies, but any human corpse on a couple of battlefields. Mortars and machine guns took care of them just as easy as a spell.

I did not have a machine gun or mortar with me this time.

"Inglorious Bastards," I shouted and zinged off a spell from each hand.

The spells zipped through a zombie each and disengaged them. I kept it going, zing, zing, zing while Hannah led us backwards up the road.

I got sixteen before the first one got through. If you don't get a head shot, they keep coming. Try hitting that bullseye while they lumber toward you.

And you're running.

Backwards.

I thought I was doing pretty good.

One grabbed Hannah and she screamed.

I popped its head off.

Seven to go.

"There are more down here," said Elvis.

Dang it, I did not want to hear that.

"I said, there are more down here!" he shouted.

I must have said it out loud. I popped off a couple of more heads.

"Hannah!" I screamed. "Get us to a trolley."

She rushed us up a side street. My precog kicked in. I ducked and rolled as a spell ricocheted off the iron fence beside me.

I heard the witch cackle, but couldn't see her in the dark.

"Down, down!" I shouted.

Hannah flattened to the ground. Elvis threw himself on top of her, lot of good that it did. It was a noble gesture from a ghost that had no impact other than to tell me what kind of man I let die under my watch.

That made me want to save Hannah even more. I had a new rule. No more good people die while I'm around.

I heard the witch shuffle up ahead in the darkness, and the footfalls of the Haitian zombies as they trudged up the street.

I drew in a deep breath, thought the spell, one in each hand and let fly.

"Raging Bull!"

A force of will shot in each direction of the alley. I heard the witch scream before she threw up a counter spell. The Zombies had no protection. My will disintegrated them, leaving only the dusty bones of their feet on the road.

The witch had disappeared.

I limped over to Hannah.

"Are you okay?"

She shivered as I lifted her through Elvis.

"Sorry," I said.

"That tickled," Elvis told us.

"I'm okay. Did you get them all?"

She looked over my shoulder at the fourteen feet planted across the asphalt.

"That's going to cause questions," she said.

"We'll have to take care of it later," I told her. "First, get me to the cemetery so I can shut it up."

"And then?"

"Then we find the witch, stop her monster, and kill the warlock hunting for us."

"Tuesday," said Elvis. "We call that Tuesday."

19

CHAPTER NINETEEN

The trolley dropped us three blocks from her beetle and they stumbled along the sidewalk just as millions of other NOLA revelers before them.

I held up Hannah with an arm over her shoulders, partially to help her straight and partially to anchor her to reality.

It's not every day an academic goes up against a horde of zombies and lives to record the tale. It shook her up.

I could tell.

She was literally shaking in my arms.

"That was intense," she said in a low rasp.

Maybe more stirred up than shaken.

"It usually is," I answered.

"They kept coming at us, and you were blasting and zapping. Is magic always so silent?"

"It can be," I said. "The more you train, the quieter you can be."

"He made noise," she said. "And he had a wand."

I knew both.

Even though the Judge trained us to use our minds, it wasn't always easy. Part of the training is learning to ignore a million years of evolution that has kept humanity surviving.

Things like fear, and the adrenal dump that goes with it. The heart rate pops up, pumping blood where it needs to be for flight or fight. Eyes go wide so you can better take in your surroundings. Limbs twitch because fear makes you want to move, a primal urge to instant reaction.

It's why so many people jump when they get startled.

They scream to warn others.

All built into our DNA and the Judge thought it was his job to recode it.

The old Marshal of the West was still learning.

I had a couple of decades on him.

But his wands were awesome.

Two of them built into the barrels of antique Colt revolvers. Showoff.

A shadow detached from a wall as we approached and sparks drizzled from the tip of my finger.

"Hold Marshal," said a voice I recognized.

Claude stepped into the glowing light from a streetlamp and held up both hands.

"I come in peace," he said.

I squeezed Hannah's shoulder and shifted her half behind me, out of the way should anything happen.

"Skulking in the dark," I said to him. "Kind of a cliché from the book Lestat."

He smiled, humor making his pale face incandescent in the

solar LED.

"That damn book," he snickered. "Fun reading but I shall send you something more substantial to expand your literary horizons."

"Thanks," I told him. "How's the conclave?"

He glanced at Hannah, then shrugged.

"The Hawks call for war, the doves sue for coexistence. It is as it has always been."

"Which one are you?"

I couldn't help but glance over my shoulder to search for threats. The first batch of zombies might have been gone, but Phyllis was still out there.

"I am a realist," said the vampire. "As real as one can be having lived as long as I have."

"You're a vampire," a voice squeaked from behind me.

"Hello, my dear," Claude vamped up the charm. "We haven't been introduced."

"Stop it," I warned him.

Claude sighed.

"I am afraid it is a defense mechanism Marshal. On my honor I mean neither of you harm."

"I'm the Watcher," Hannah chirped, emboldened by my defense and the blood still racing through her veins.

I bet it was practically singing to the vampire.

"That is a good thing to mean," I said. "Let me return the favor. I caught a ride with a Normanii into town after I left you in the train."

His sharp intake of breath spoke volumes.

"The Northmen are here," he seemed distracted. "This puts a new spin on the chatter I am hearing."

I could have asked for more. Hell, if I wasn't on a witch hunt I would have. But vampire's conclave a lot. The infighting among the clans is legendary and creatures of immense power were always jockeying for more.

Half of being a vampire that survived was learning the politics of it. Probably more important than blood.

"Then let me repay the kindness of your warning with one of my own," he said, dark eyes glittering. "The monster you seek has joined the witch you fought. You know they are in New Orleans, but do not know where yet. I will discover this and share it with you."

"That is a kindness," I told him.

"You have given me information far more valuable," he said. "I only came to warn you of their partnership. Now I must do more to even the scales."

Part of blood sucking politics was the trading of favors. Vamps hated owing anybody.

"Alright," I agreed because you just don't turn down that kind of help when it's offered.

Claude turned and disappeared without a good bye or by your leave. I wondered if I should live as long as he, would I have forgot the niceties too?

"Did you just make a deal with a vampire?"

Hannah shifted in front of me.

"Wait until we get to your place," I answered. "I wanted the wards between us and what else might be out there."

And a beer.

I really wanted a beer.

Kicking zombie butt and politicking with vamps was thirsty business.

20

CHAPTER TWENTY

Hannah parked her beetle in the covered garage accessed through an automatic gate. The previous Marshal did good work on the wards, the car slid through with just a small stutter in the engine.

Some of the patterns made more sense now that I knew he had a relationship with this woman.

She kicked off her boots as soon as we stepped through the door and returned with two Abita. I took one from her, twisted off the top and drank a couple of sips before plopping on the sofa.

"Got any aspirin?"

She nodded and smiled, disappeared into the rear of the home. I listened as she moved from room to room, lights clicking on and off.

"If you can't find some, never mind," I called out and used

one foot to shuck off a boot l, then the other.

I nudged them under the sofa and she returned, dressed in pj's and a robe.

She held out her hand and dropped four white pills into mine.

"I found them," she said. "I just wanted to get more comfortable."

Comfort sounded like something I needed to so I settled back further into the couch and treated my beer on my hip.

"Do you want to talk about tonight?"

I want to drink about tonight," she said and did just that.

She finished hers first, waited for me to drain mine and then took our empties back into the kitchen to replace them.

She came back and sat on the couch opposite me.

"One more of these and I'll be tipsy," she giggled and locked eyes with new as she put the bottle to her lips.

"Two is my limit," I wiggled the bottle at her and earned a pout.

"That's no fun," she said. "Doesn't almost being killed make you appreciate being alive?"

"I do," I took a sip. "I am. Good beer. Good company. Good fire."

I drilled a shot into the kindling under the stacked logs in the fireplace setting a small blaze crackling.

She snuggled into the cushions and stared at the flames.

"I've never lost anyone I've loved before," she said after the silence stretched out in a comfortable distance.

"I have. It's not easy."

"No," she said. "He would never take me out on the job though."

"Part of his job is keeping you safe."

"He did. He took all of it seriously."

I wasn't sure who she was trying to convince.

"You're different from him."

"I'm a different person."

"Your magic." she adjusted so she could face me. "It's different. It was like watching a wild animal."

"He had more control," I said.

"It wasn't just that. My dad was in the army and took me to a range growing up. That's how I learned to shoot. Have you ever seen a. 50 Cal?"

"I was in the Army," I nodded.

"You were? Small world. Then you know the difference between a .45 sidearm and a .50 Cal rifle."

I nodded.

"You're the rifle," she said.

"Being aimed by a monkey," Elvis chimed in.

I looked over and saw him mesmerized by the dancing flames in the hearth.

"Why do you do that," she asked.

I felt her shift closer.

"Why do you look like there's someone there?"

Because there was. A young guy, just like you, who believed I could keep him safe and failed, I said in my mind.

"Is it a ghost?" She asked and I turned my head.

She was close to my face.

"Do the memories haunt you too?"

She leaned in and kissed me. Just for a moment, I almost let her.

She was soft, and warm and there, hopped up and excited by her brush with death, and I was hungry for the touch of a woman.

My blood was singing.

It was roaring as it pounced through my ears.

She could feel my strong heartbeat in her pain as she put her hand on my chest and it must have excited her more.

I pulled back after three seconds.

Maybe four and even then it was close.

"I have a wife," I said.

She scooted away.

"I'm so sorry," she stammered. "There isn't a ring and..."

"I know," my turn to stammer. "She's been missing for a couple of years."

"Oh. How many?"

"Ten."

"Ten years?"

"Yes."

"And you're holding out hope she's coming back?"

I drained the second beer and rubbed my hand on the back of my neck.

"I did go on a date a while ago."

"So you're getting back out there?"

"She ended up being an evil witch summoning demons to earth, I confessed. The ones I'm hunting now."

That made her laugh and she hopped off the couch. I watched her cute pert little I'm not gonna touch it butt sashay into the kitchen and come back with a couple of bottles.

We killed a sixer, she passed one to me and curled up in the leather chair.

"Can't abandon the last two in the fridge."

I twisted the top and drank slowly.

"You know what I appreciate about you Marshal?"

She looked at the fire again.

"You don't do things half measure. Don't date for a decade

and when you do, she's an arch nemesis."

"Not my arch nemesis," I joked. "That's a Sicilian when deathbed on the line."

That earned an air toast.

"You know you could have spent the night in my bed and used the missing wife as an excuse in the morning. "

"That wouldn't be right," I said and kind of felt regret that I didn't think of it.

"A boy scout."

"They weren't around when I was growing up. But the sentiment was the same."

She grinned, finished her beer and this time left the empties on the end table.

"I'm going to bed," she announced and stood at the end of the sofa. "If you get cold, or scared...or lonely, feel free to join me."

She left before I could answer.

"Should you stay or should you go now?" Elvis sang.

Damn it. No matter what I decided, I wasn't getting much sleep tonight.

21

CHAPTER TWENTY ONE

"There's someone out there," Elvis whispered in my ear.

Panic. The best alarm clock ever.

I bolted off the sofa and stared at the door.

"Where?"

The embers from last night's fire still glowed in the hearth, a soft red glow leaking across the floor and casting weird shadows from the stacks of books.

"Some guy at the fence. He can't come through."

I went over to the window and peeked through the thick curtains. A shadowed figure stood by the gate and stared at the house.

"It's not Claude," said the ghost.

Shorter. Thicker. And human.

I stepped through the front door onto the cool planks for the front porch.

A thrall. I could tell by the eyes, the far away look that vampire hypnosis created.

"I can't come in," he said in a frat boy bubble voice.

I queued up a spell, just in case he was a distraction and stepped down to the fence.

"Watch my back," I said to Elvis in a soft voice.

"Wards," he reminded me.

I didn't remind him that he was cowering behind wards when a couple of witches came calling to kill him.

The thrall watched me approach, looking like a Goth and Stoner got together to make his outfit. Long unkempt hair dyed black around a pale face that hadn't seen sunlight in years. Loose baggie pajama bottoms, black to match the mood, and a black tank top completed his look. Even black sandals on his feet, yellow toenails in need of trimming.

"Nice eyes," I told him.

They were rimmed with black, an attempt to turn them into soulless pits of despair. It ended up looking like clown make up.

Guess he didn't expect a compliment.

"Thanks dude."

There it was. Dude. Hippie stoner all the way. Nailed it. I expected the Scooby gang to pull up in a mystery machine any moment.

"If you can't come in, you want me to come out and play?"

I twirled my index finger in the air.

He actually backed up, and tripped off the curb, fell flat on his ass in the street, black eyes blinking in panic.

"No man, no way."

I took a step forward to help him up and he cringed.

"I'm just here with a message man," he said with the words

almost running together. "Claude sent me."

I stopped and figured I would just hold tight before me trying to help killed the poor guy.

"What do you have for me?"

He took his time getting up, brushing off the bottom of the flowing pj's.

"An address," he said. "But he didn't tell me what it was for."

I held out a hand.

He took a double take at the extended index finger and stepped to one side as he approached the gate. I could reach through the wards with just the slightest tingle in my forearm.

He put a folded piece of elegant stationary in my hand and jumped back.

"That it?"

The thrall nodded.

"You got a home to go to?"

More nodding.

"Then get gone."

I pulled my arm back in and almost heard the spiritual pop of the ward resealing once I was through. We watched the kid run down the street and slip around the corner.

"Do you think it's the blood that makes them cattle, or is it the drugs that make them easier prey?" Elvis observed from above me.

I turned and found him floating head down.

"I think it's a combo."

He nodded, chin bobbing up to his chest.

"There a reason you're floating that way?"

I walked back toward the house. The ghost let the tether tug him along rather than expend any energy floating.

"The vampire thrall has me thinking about blood," he said. "If I hang upside down, the blood will rush to my head."

I paused on the porch and stared at him.

"Do ghosts have blood?"

He screwed up his eyes and lifted until we were eye to eye again, his mouth talking into my forehead, the bells of his bellbottoms disappearing into the wood slats of the roof.

"You know, I don't know," he answered. "If you cut me, do I not bleed."

"I can't cut a ghost."

"Not even with magic?"

I shrugged.

"Never tried."

"I can't remember if I ever read it," he took a deep breath, held it and shot it through his nose. I didn't feel a breeze, nothing. Ghosts don't really breathe, Elvis was just mimicking the memory of what he used to do automatically.

"I don't know if I knew it before and can't recall it, or if I never researched it in the first place. Have we dealt with ghosts before?"

I shook my head.

"Not many, and I never asked you to look that up. It wouldn't have crossed my mind to search for ghost blood."

He rolled around in the air and floated back to his normal spot, just a little taller than me because his feet didn't touch the ground.

"It was a long shot," he said.

I dragged the sad pitiful spirit into the house.

Hannah waited, a steaming mug of coffee in each hand. She passed one to me.

"Nectar of the gods," she grinned over the rim and sipped

the clarifying liquid.

"If you only knew how right you were," I said sipping my own.

I have a passion for craft beer, but coffee is an addiction. The love affair went back to my youth, when work on the orphanage farm was expected if we wanted to eat.

Back then, coffee and kids went together just as well as adults, without all the annoying lectures from medical establishments about the effects of caffeine on growing bodies.

The Father liked his coffee black, strong enough to eat a hole in the stomach, and hot enough to keep the local fire brigade on standby. It was like pouring electricity in the vein, and allowed a group of kids to get a lot of chores done before lessons.

I carried that addiction through the Army and the Sidhe War, and every morning I was able since.

She made a good cup. Black like I liked it, but there was a hint of something extra.

"Chicory," she said as she noticed the appreciation on my face.

I gave her a grin and finished half the cup.

"Coffee was a gift from the gods," I told her.

If I hoped to impress her with my smarts, she wasn't having it. She probably was one cup ahead of me on the joe anyway, because if I had a full cup of that chicory laced delish in my belly, I would have realized she was a reader, and the tomes scattered around the room covered a lot of different topics.

"One of the legends of Prometheus is he stole coffee and gave it to man, not fire," her eyes sparkled in mischief.

"Coffee is fire in the veins if you do it right," I shot back. "This weak stuff you serve is good for you lightweights."

She smirked in mock irritation and slugged my bicep, spilling coffee onto the folded stationary in my hand.

"Oops," she said.

She reached out and took the coffee mug from me.

"If you don't like it, there's a shop up the street. Serves mud, but if you're like my dad, that's what you army guys like."

I flicked my fingers and magicked the cup back into my fist.

"I'll finish this first since I'm your guest. It's only polite."

"No fair," she swatted me again.

This time I managed to keep the coffee in the cup, then in my mouth as I carried it and the paper over by the fireplace.

I put the mug on the mantle and unfolded the sheet of thick paper. It looked old, fashionable when Dickens was using the inkwell to tell tales of two cities and paid a pound per word.

The script was neat and elegant.

"Penmanship is a lost art," Elvis sighed as he read over my shoulder.

"What does it say?" the Watcher asked me from the other side. "Do you feel a draft in here? I can stoke the fire."

"I'm fine," I told her. "It's just an address to check on later tonight."

"The Vampire?"

I nodded.

"Do you trust him."

I had to think about that. Trust was a funny thing when it came to the spirit world. In most instances, someone's word was law, and promises irrevocable on pain of intense retribution.

And vampires had the whole favor layer factored in.

"Trust?" I waved my hand back and forth in a see saw motion. "But verify."

A sealed envelope slid under the door with a slight scratch.

CHAPTER TWENTY ONE

We both stared at it for a moment, shocked.

"The wards?" she said.

I ran to the door and yanked it open, a spell ready to blast whatever creature had managed to make it through her protection spells.

But the porch was empty.

So was the yard. And the street beyond.

Hannah bent to retrieve the paper and I stopped her.

"It could be cursed," I said and sent a feeler toward it.

There was a hint of magic, but like a dusting left in someone passing. The envelope itself was not inherently magic.

"It's clean," I said and snapped my fingers.

The envelope floated up on a breeze and I caught it.

"Cool trick."

I pulled the wax seal holding the edges together. NOLA was full of mysteries, the least of not which was how were so many still using archaic traditions to communicate. Two missives scratched on stationary, one hand delivered by a messenger, one with a wax seal I didn't know delivered by a mystery.

It was from the Gnome.

"Knu wants to see me," I told Hannah and handed her the two words scratched on a cream colored card stock.

"It just says COME."

"I get the point."

I went back to the sofa and fished out my boots to slip on. Hannah refilled my coffee in a to go cup.

"Want me to drive?"

I shook my head.

"The walk will do me good."

I took the coffee from her, but she didn't let it go right away.

"I want to thank you for last night," she ducked her head, a blush creeping up her cheeks.

"We didn't do anything last night."

"Yes, but I wanted to. I know it's not very ladylike, but," she chewed on her lip. "I was lonely and wanted to feel something, and my mom says I've got this whole power thing fetish."

I didn't know what to say, so she kept going.

"You could have taken advantage of the way I was feeling, and I wanted you to, but I'm glad you didn't. Does that make sense?"

I shook my head.

She harrumphed.

"I know, it doesn't make sense to me either. To want something and to be glad it didn't happen. But there it is. And well, I just wanted to say thank you."

"You're welcome."

"If you come back tonight, I'll try not to be so bold."

I waved the vampire's note in hand, and stuck it in the pocket of my bomber as I slipped it on, juggling the coffee.

"Meeting tonight."

"Need me for back up?"

"Watchers need to be protected," Elvis said.

She shivered.

"I'll get you if I do."

Hannah curled her arms around her shoulders and squeezed.

"I'm going to have to check for leaks in the doors and windows today," she shivered again.

"I think it's going to get warmer today. Might not matter," I told her, trying to save her some time.

She leaned in, kissed me on the cheek as I walked out of the front door and popped through the wards at the fence.

22

CHAPTER TWENTY TWO

The thrall showed up before the sun did which meant I was out of the door and heading toward the Gnome's place as the sun rose. It was one of my favorite times of the day, and the walk was pleasant through the stirring streets of a city with over two hundred years of history.

I remembered legends of New Orleans from my youth, jazz clubs and razors in boots, Cajun prostitutes and a mélange of different cultures washed up on the muddy banks of the Mississippi River.

I could see hints of it in the architecture, each block influenced by a different time and place, and some of it so modern it created a bridge to the past.

By the time the big orange ball dribbled in the horizon and sent blasts of burning magic across the landscape, I was in front of Knu's shop.

The door was open and she was waiting for me.

"You didn't bring me any?" she indicated the cup.

I turned it upside down to show her it was empty.

"You took long enough to arrive," she shut the shop behind her and led me back into the street.

"I came as soon as I got the note?"

She snorted.

"That damn pixie," she laughed. "I sent her hours ago."

Pixies were notorious for being flighty, both in a literal and figurative sense. Give a pixie a task, and if they stayed on it, the thing could be done in a flash.

Send that same pixie past something shiny and you could lose your timetable just as fast.

The Gnome knew how her messenger would react. Probably even did some scrying to see when the note would pop under the door.

"I had a visit from a thrall before sunup," I told her, even though I would bet she already knew. "The pixie was playing it safe."

"Meeting at midnight?"

She said it as a question, but it was more like a confirmation of something she had seen before.

I nodded.

"It's not going to be easy," she warned me and said as much as she dared share.

The problem with the future for someone who knows it is easily summed up with the story of the merchant in a Middle Eastern bazaar who sees death near his stall.

Death reacts, startled to see the man, and so to escape his fate, he takes off on a horse and rides it to death to another city.

That night, he sees Death in the city and says, "I can't escape.

You've got me. But tell me why you reacted at my stall?"

And Death answered, "Because I had an appointment to collect you here tonight and I was surprised to see you there."

Or as I like to put it.

There is no fate but what you make.

If you know what you're doing. The trouble was, no one really knew what they were doing, as far as the future was concerned. A good intention today turns into an unforeseen repercussion downstream.

Prohibitionists wanted to save America's soul, and created a gang war that built the mafia and killed hundreds of thousands in the decades since.

Good idea. Bad execution.

Scratch that, anyone who wanted to outlaw beer was a soulless demon, probably in the employ of the Sidhe.

So bad idea, worse execution.

But I would bet every single one of those hypocritical teetotalers would have said, "Nah, forget it," if they knew shoving their morals down from a high horse would kill so many people later.

Or maybe not.

People were strange.

"Easy like Sunday morning," Elvis hummed.

"Reminds me of something," I told Knu. "Heard of any way to help a ghost keep his memories?"

"Your friend is slipping away?"

"There might not be any hope for him," I said glancing at him. "But I thought I'd ask."

"I'll look into it," she said and kept striding for our destination.

"Got to have faith, faith, faith," sang Elvis.

Knu took us to one side of a famous café that bypassed the tourists and knocked on a window. It slid open and she passed a ten through, got two large cups of coffee in return.

"Locals only," she winked and passed me a cup.

We carried them to Crescent park on the edge of the Mississippi River and sat across from each other at a picnic table as the morning kept waking up around us.

She let it be pleasant for a few moments, then took a deep breath, a sip of coffee and we got down to business.

23

CHAPTER TWENTY THREE

"I'm going to tell you something and it's going to blow your mind

hole."

Her eyes sparkled across from me at the picnic table. We could see tugs and barges chugging past from here, the noise abated by the distance and some strategically placed reeds along the banks that acted as sound absorbers.

The morning sun was bright, but we could see ugly grey clouds squatting to the horizon, the threat of a tropical storm churning off the coast.

Bad juju, I knew.

Something was stirring up the water.

"My mind hole is ready to be blown," I assured her.

After our last adventure together, when I saved her from mortal mafia assassins, I chalked Knu into the friend column, which was surprisingly light. I could tick off her, a Valkyrie and the dead ghost hanging out by my shoulder in that category.

The not friend's column was a whole lot longer.

"The world of magic is a lot different than you think," she said.

I nodded.

I was a young pup in the world of magic, only almost a hundred. I bet this tiny little woman had me by a couple of centuries.

She smiled and the skin around her eyes crinkled.

"Ten times that," she said.

That kinda did blow my mind a little. I had to remember she could read minds if she wanted to. It was part of her act in the French Quarter, but all of her magic.

At least the part I knew about. If she was a couple of thousand years old, there was a lot I didn't know.

It also meant I was sitting in front of some super-duper power in an itty-bitty package.

"You don't look a day over a thousand," I said.

Her pupils widened a little and a real smile slip the creased on her cheek revealing strong teeth, even if a little yellowed. She cackled.

"I didn't see that coming," she slapped the table. "No wonder the Judge likes you."

"He doesn't show it," I said.

She glanced up at the storm clouds.

"He wouldn't."

The smile slid off her face, though traces of it made her eyes twinkle in the twilight colored air around us.

"You would be surprised at how old I truly am, and yet I am young compared to some."

"It's all relative," I told her.

"No, I'm not related to anyone," she shot back. "No one left alive at least."

I almost told her I was joking but Elvis saved me.

"She's joking," he whispered in my ear.

She saw the goosebumps tickle the skin on my arm from that side of my body and snorted.

"The ghost is giving away all my good stuff."

"He's always been a little quick on the uptake. When he can remember."

"I recall," she said. "Now as to the knowledge that will blow your mind, give me your hand."

I reached across the table, palms up, expecting her to take a look at my lifeline. There were scars on the skin of each, cutting through the lines in several places.

As I expected, she studied them, then placed her hands in mine, intertwining our fingers and clamping tight.

"People might think we're going steady," I grinned. "I'm a bit old fashioned."

"Out of time and place," she nodded. "Welcome to the life I live."

Her grip grew tighter and hotter where our skin touched.

Under different circumstances, I would have tossed up a shield and a lightning bolt, but like I said, I knew this gnome from a long time ago. I trusted her.

"Your world is going to shatter," she warned me. "There is great pain coming for you."

Fantastic.

Nothing works up the old confidence level like prognostications of doom.

"The things you think you know are wrong. The things that

you must learn are false. And when the time comes, you must decide."

She relaxed her grip but didn't let go of my hands.

"I know that doesn't help. The future is flexible and mostly malleable. Think of all the decisions you make in one day that have an impact downstream. Turn left instead of right, get hit by a bus. Order delivery instead of going out, and you get food poisoning."

"There is no fate but what we make."

Her eyes widened.

"That is a good way to approach the task before you."

"I saw it in a movie," I told her.

Didn't want the mind reader to think I was taking credit for somebody else's bumper sticker platitude.

"Close your eyes," she said.

I did.

"Are you going to kiss me?" I teased.

"Something like that."

I didn't feel warm wet senior citizen lips on mine, though I might have liked it.

What I felt was a spinning vortex that whirled around us and though I was scared and ready to fight, I kept my eyes closed.

"Trust, remember."

"Open," she commanded.

We were in a glade staring at a line of half naked men brandishing clubs, bronze swords and skin shields. Some were on horseback, directing the others, like generals or commanders of some sort.

Not the sort I was used to dealing with.

When I was in the Great War, or Sidhe War as I truly knew it, my role started as a soldier in the infantry. The generals I knew stayed way behind friendly lines, far from the fight and potential to be killed in battle.

These guys did not get that memo.

Their generals and leaders were not only in the fray, but at the front of it.

"Why are they fighting?"

"That's not fighting," the gnome said from beside me. "That's training."

I glanced back at the men on the field, and the strewn bodies leading up to the line.

Most of them were still moving, albeit slow.

"Watch," she directed me to look at a man on horseback riding along the outside of the advancing line.

He led the horse toward us in an attempt to flank the group, and a quarter of the men along that side angled toward him to counter his attack.

"It's a ruse," I said and sure enough, the horseman was a distraction.

As soon as the line turned to fight him, the opposition rushed in and crashed into their now exposed flank.

The man on horseback slowed to a trot and pulled up just in front of where we were standing.

He was tall for the time, half naked like the others, wearing only a plain spun wrap around his waist, sandals strapped to his feet and muscular calves and paint on his chest. He looked like a Spartan warrior from the movie where they fought the Persians.

Ripped, muscular, tan and angry.

He glared at the men and screamed.

I couldn't understand the words coming out of his mouth.

"A form of Gaelic," the Gnome said. "We don't have to

whisper. What you are observing is a memory."

"When is this?"

"Five thousand years before you were born? More maybe? The records of this history are long gone and buried."

"Then how do you know it?"

"Magic," she said.

Which could explain a lot. Or was just her way of deflecting the question.

The voice of the General sounded familiar, but I wasn't sure if that was because I had been on the receiving end of yells like that before, or it was just his voice.

There are only so many tonal qualities and pitches in the human range, and though his words were lost to me, the meaning was clear.

Get your ass in gear and get your act together.

The gnome reached her fingers up in front of my face and snapped her fingers.

Like a switch, the volume didn't change, but the words did.

"I don't give a frog's ass if you're tired," the General screamed. "Do you think the fekkin' fairies are going to give a damn if you're ready for your supper?!"

I was right, he was laying into the group of men.

The battle had fizzled out in front of us as he yelled, the men looked exhausted and spent.

"What are they preparing for?"

"War," the gnome answered. "Why else train?"

She was right.

If this was five thousand years ago, they would be preparing to battle another clan or invaders. I tried to remember my history. Were Vikings around that long ago? Who was?

I guess it depended on where we were and when.

I looked around at the landscape trying to place it, but if you've ever tried to figure out where you were by just the look of the trees and bushes around you, it ain't always easy.

Sure, if there were cactus, you could guess Arizona, or lots of alpine trees, and you could guess Switzerland.

This valley looked like a thousand other meadows I'd seen on three continents. Long narrow pasture, trees on either side, leading to a small rise on the end I could see.

The grass was filled with clover, which kept it mostly shin high on the soldiers training beyond, but that could have been a result of feet that stamped through the field all day and tramped it down.

The General nudged his horse forward.

"We'll do it again," he called out.

The men grumbled and gathered their weapons to separate into two sections on either end of the field. As they went, they gathered the fallen, helping some back into battle stances, and carting others off to the side where they could recuperate.

"Look," said the gnome and pointed a gnarled finger to a spot in the bushes several yards from us.

The leaves rustled and parted as two tiny three foot tall figures stepped out of the shadows behind the general. They were dressed much as he was, bare-chested and kilted, and so perfectly formed that it made me catch my breath.

They looked like children, but held bows in one hand, swords on their hips and attitudes like they were a couple of bad asses on the prowl.

We watched the duo saunter toward the General. The one in the back hesitated and stared at the bushes we were standing in.

"Can they see us?" I whispered.

The gnome shook her head.

"We are but ghosts here, observing, but he may sense some-thing. His power is great."

"Power?" I said and looked around for Elvis.

My own personal pet ghost was nowhere to be found, and I felt a twinge. It was the first time we'd been separated since I got him killed by a couple of witches in Memphis.

I knew the Gnome beside me was powerful, but my estimation shot up a couple of notches. Making a memory ghost was something no one else could do.

Maybe the Judge.

Then it kicked me in the nuts.

I realized why I knew that voice so well and stared at the man on horseback.

"Judge," I said.

"Not bad for a babe," Knu giggled. "I mean infant, not the kind like him."

She pointed.

The muscles in his back rippled as he held the reins, the corded legs clenched the girth of the horse, clamping him down tight. His other hand rested on the pommel of a sword, and he wore a leather thong around his neck with an iron totem carved in a symbol I didn't know.

The two tiny men approached him and he caught the move-ment from the corner of his eye.

"Go home boys," he shouted. "There's no room for children in this fight."

"Children?" said the little one in the lead.

They stopped several steps away from the horse.

"Saddle me not with infants!" the Judge screamed.

The lead man leaped from the ground and flipped in the air.

He sent three arrows winging from his bow to a spot in the field and landed on the flanks of the Judge's horse.

A tiny needle tipped knife pressed against the Judge's tender neck as the little man curled his hair in his small fist and yanked back.

"I am no infant," the small man growled. "Nor am I a child to be sent home."

The Judge didn't flinch.

He didn't move either, which told me something, but I couldn't see fear on his face.

"This is where the munchkin gets turned into a pile of ash," I whispered.

"Not yet."

The Judge laughed.

It echoed across the field and caught the attention of the soldiers who gathered around the horse in a semi-circle.

"You'll have to forgive me one of the wee," the Judge said. "I was mistaken in my rush to dismiss and did not pay attention to who made the approach."

The wee one lowered his dagger and bowed.

I guess the apology worked.

He leaped off the back of the horse with an impressive flip and landed on light feet next to his partner. They stared up at the Judge in expectation.

He slid off the back of the horse and kneeled in front of them and waited until they did a quick bow.

"Easily forgiven," said the second one as he held out a hand. "I am Radar of Clan Riley, come to join you in your fight. And you've met Shannon of Clan Dell."

The Judge glanced at the three arrows sticking into the one inch ball of iron on the pommel of the sword stuck in the ground a hundred yards away.

"You are most welcome in our fight," he rose.

"Not just your fight against the First Folk," said Shannon.

His fingers worked the hilt of his dagger like he was playing a flute.

"Aye," the Judge agreed. "This is a fight for all of our world."

"Who are the First Folk?" I asked. "And who are the munchkins?"

Radar turned to face the bush and studied it with keen eyes, eyebrows crinkled in concentration.

"Are you sure he can't see us?"

"See us? No. He senses us though," said the Gnome.

"Let me guess. Magic."

She nodded.

"Do you not know what they are?"

I studied them closer. They had sun weathered skin, freckles and looked as if they could be cousins.

"Clans," I said. "Scots?"

"Close. Wrong island."

"Irish," I said. "Celts."

"Even before there was a name for Celts, these are those people."

"Which ones? The Judge or the little people."

Radar stomped over to the bush and parted the leaves. I could have reached out and tweaked his nose he was so close.

He peered left and right, up and down, looking right over and through us. He even sniffed long and deep, as if he could catch our scents.

"What do you sense?"

Shannon joined him, dagger in hand.

"I cannot tell," Radar huffed. "Something."

CHAPTER TWENTY THREE

"What is it Wee Folk?"

"He senses something, but knows not what," Shannon explained.

The Judge made a motion with his hands and scouts went to either side of the woods and began hunting, searching.

"You think the Sidhe sent a spy?"

Shannon nodded.

"They always have spies," he spat.

"Then let us away to my camp," the Judge said. "You are my guests."

Shannon nodded as if he expected nothing less.

"Who are these guys?" I whispered.

Radar drew his sword and shoved it into the bushes. The point slid into my chest, but didn't leave a mark.

That didn't mean it didn't hurt though.

I grunted.

I'd been stabbed before, but last time there was a lot of blood. This time, it was just a dull ache, like a piece of ice inside of me.

He did it again and I almost punched the little turd nugget.

"Did you get it?" Shannon asked.

The tiny man shook his head.

"Nothing," he said confused. "There is nothing there."

It didn't feel like nothing.

It felt like getting stabbed with an icicle.

I wanted to punch him. But I figured it wouldn't do me a lot of good.

"It would not," the Gnome agreed.

We watched the Judge hop up on the back of the horse and scoot forward, making room for Shannon and Radar to join him.

They leaped up behind him, settled in as he galloped over the rise and out of view.

"So the Judge, huh?"

She nodded.

"There is still more to learn."

I rubbed the cold spot on my chest.

"I'm okay so long as people quit stabbing me with tiny ghost swords."

"Stop making them nervous," she said.

"Me? What did I do? I asked a question. We're in the spirit world, right? He can't hear me in the spirit world."

"Magic," she said. "And theirs is the oldest. You don't know what they're capable of."

Her watery eyes stared into mine.

"Then why don't you tell me?"

So she did.

24

CHAPTER TWENTY FOUR

We popped up on the edge of a campsite in a clearing in the woods. I could see pickets in the trees around us, sentries staring into the growing darkness for enemies that preferred the cover of night.

Knu directed my eyes inward to a fire flickering in a pit. Logs were placed around the fire for seating, and the Judge and his men sat on them filling cups with red liquid from a goatskin sack.

Shannon and Riley sat on one side of him, watching the men with equal parts amusement and curiosity.

"Leprechauns," Knu said and I saw her eyes glisten with unshed tears as she stared at the two tiny men. "They are cousins of my people."

Gnomes and Leprechauns in the same branch? I shook my head and started to point out the differences.

"It is," she stated with a finality that shut me up. "All of what you call the wee ones, the little people are of the same tribe of Fairie. Pixies, Gnomes, Leprechauns, Sprites, Imps and more."

Hobbits? I almost asked.

But the sadness in her face made me hold my voice.

"Did you know them?" I asked instead.

She nodded.

"In this world before the bridge was torn asunder, many of the Folk travelled back and forth. The leprechauns settled on this island, while my people moved into the Black Forest."

The history of our world was an evolution in information. It's something most people take for granted, especially today when so much of our daily lives are recorded and captured, and stored.

People don't realize that a daily record is a relatively recent phenomenon.

Newspaper dailies lasted for just over a century, and prior to that, information was done through weekly papers, and even those have only been around for a couple of hundred years before that.

The thing about recorded history is for the longest time, it wasn't.

There were oral traditions, and stories passed down, but so much has been lost, that it's hard to know what is true, what is fiction and what is a mixture of the two.

Even modern history can be wrong.

Everyone has seen the DEWEY WINS ELECTION headline, a misprint that was plain wrong. But if something happens, and that image is the one that happens to survive a thousand years, people then will construct a narrative around Dewey winning a presidency.

"You need to tell me about the bridge," I said. "And the Black Forest."

One was information I could use to fight the Sidhe, or at least tell the Judge, though by the looks of the warrior in front of us, he might know it already. The second was my own curiosity.

Plus, I noticed she didn't say how she knew them.

And it looked like she wasn't going to. Her eyes were locked on the three figures by the fire in a really easy to decipher pay attention look.

So I did.

As far as we think we've advanced in technology, knowledge and our understanding of the world, I don't know that any modern man would react so nonchalant about creatures of legend walking out of the woods to join a fight. The Judge sat on one of the fallen logs dragged around the fire and ladled stew onto his trencher, and invited the guests to help themselves before tucking in with a chunk of bread.

The leprechauns heaped oversized portions of thick peppery stew onto trenchers of their own, and skipped the bread, opting to scoop with two fingers and shovel it into tiny mouths.

The rest of the men settled into spots, all close enough to hear and share voice, and I realized I'd seen this before.

Not this particular tableau, but one so close like it that only the men and uniforms changed. It was a council of war, and the Judge was giving his men time to recover, unwind and decompress before they made further plans. The appearance of the wee one's, though unexpected, must have been a boon to their fight.

Radar finished first, licking the smooth wood trencher clean before wiping it with the elbow of his sleeve and placing it back by the kettle. He searched around for a moment, and the Judge slipped a rope knotted skin off his shoulder and held it out to him. The leprechaun uncapped it, smelled the liquid and squirted a long pull into his mouth.

He recapped it and tossed it to Shannon, who repeated the action, and kept it.

The Judge smiled.

There were obligations as host he was obliged to follow, and once the tiny warriors were fed, and thirst addressed, he could turn the conversation to business.

No matter that only the sounds of men smacking and knives scraping against wood competed with the crackling of the fire as the light pressed back the growing darkness.

"You're magic," I sighed to Knu. "Couldn't you just have poofed us to the good part? What does their eating have to do with anything?"

Radar spun around like a top, bow raised and sent an arrow straight into my heart.

It passed through me and sent a cold shiver up my spine.

"Little shite has good aim," I remarked.

He notched two more and let fly. All flew true and through me, three arrows planted in a one inch circle on the tree behind us.

"We all do," she whispered.

"What do you see?" Shannon asked.

"I can't say," his partner answered. "But the spirits are out there, I think. Fae spies."

"None can approach," the Judge placed his trencher in the pile and wiped his hands on the cloth around his waist. "The ways are warded.

But he made a signal and the men went on high alert, searching for the enemy the wee one hunted.

CHAPTER TWENTY FOUR

"Bah on your wards," Radar spat. "The Sidhe care not for such things."

"I paid a shaman good wage to ward this camp," the Judge defended. "His magic is strong."

"Not strong enough," said Shannon. "It's why we came."

"The Judge isn't magic," I whispered, careful to keep my voice low.

I wasn't concerned with any of the soldiers tripping around in the bushes, I was just tired of getting shot by a leprechaun.

"He was not," Knu said. "But he became so."

"How?" I asked in wonder.

I didn't know a human could become magic, though again, I suppose it's a matter of faith. Should one study the ways and believe in it enough, then on a quantum level, it could be true.

And once it was true, it must always be true.

Perhaps the Judge just wanted magic more than anything else in this world, to aid in his fight against the interlopers.

"At great cost," said Knu.

She snapped her fingers again and the scene spun out of sight as the lights winked out.

25

CHAPTER TWENTY FIVE

"The Sidhe did not stop," she said.

The sun came up on a different day with a different view. The training ground was replaced by a verdant field outside of what looked like Edinburgh castle, high on a hilltop all alone.

There was a black rent in one of the hills opposite the castle, and the field between was chaos.

Men fought against creatures of myth and imagination. The Sidhe were tall and beautiful, almost painful to look upon, even in my memory state. A group of them sat on the back of giant unicorns sheathed in battle armor, their hooves pawing at the ground.

Two dozen or so were arrayed near the hole in the hill as creatures poured through. It wasn't a torrent, but a steady stream of Trolls, Goblins, Pixies, and Elves.

Not the good long haired fellows that were amazing with

acrobatics and bows, but long lithe creatures with six foot swords and angry red eyes.

What history we had of the elvish in my day was whitewashed fantasy, tainted by fantasy authors and bodice rippers who wanted the deadly creatures to be portrayed in a altruistic light.

Those same PR person's who turned blood sucking vampires into naughty imps no more harmful than mosquitos took one of the most deadly fighting creatures since the beginning of time and made them cookie makers, and noble creatures who followed light and justice.

I'd fought a contingent of elves once in Nagasaki at the end of the Sidhe War. A platoon of thirty had broken through the veil while we were distracted in the Black Forest.

The Judge barely poofed eighty of us there to set up a holding engagement until help could arrive.

Their numbers swelled to ninety despite our effort to inflect heavy losses.

We did.

So did they, taking our eighty defenders down to two.

We were able to stop them.

The Allies covered it up for us with a story about a hydrogen bomb after they dropped the first on Hiroshima.

But the truth was harsher than that.

Elves meant bad business for Earth.

The Judge sat astride a stallion on the far side of the field, like a conductor directing an orchestra of destruction.

He saw the Elves break through and motioned a cavalry unit to flank the Sidhe.

None survived.

"They can't win," I said to Knu.

They must have though. Because I existed in the future to

fight them again, another incursion through the veil.

Looking at the carnage below, I couldn't believe it was true.

I must have been from an alternative reality. Some other Universe parallel to this one, a place where the Judge was magic, where the Judge had the power to win against such odds.

Knu snapped and we popped over to the other side of battle, behind the Judge on his horse.

Now I could see better.

Things looked worse from here.

It wasn't just broken bodies, blood, the screaming of dying men. It was that there was so much of it.

Ten thousand men lay dead on the field, thousands more dying each minute. The Sidhe were outnumbered, but their magic and arms outclassed the Judge and his human army.

It wasn't even a delaying fight, unless the Sidhe were somehow inconvenienced at having to slip through the ich and ichor in their advance toward the castle.

I called to mind a thought and prepared to fight.

"You cannot," Knu cautioned and touched my arm.

"Bullshit," I countered. "Magic is thought and thought is reality. I can think myself real and give them help."

She shook her head and it broke my heart.

"Look at them," I screamed. "They're losing."

She nodded.

"I can't help them!"

She gripped my arm then, and I felt her strength as I crumpled to my knees.

"I. Said. No."

Size matters not.

She used her chin to indicate the direction I should look, but didn't let go of my arm.

I saw Shannon and Radar standing in ritual circles drawn in the dirt. None of the humans were anywhere near to keep the circle whole and unbroken.

What I didn't understand was the larger circle that extended around the two leprechauns and included the Judge.

No wonder he was having trouble directing the battle.

The son of a bitch was scared and hiding behind a shield made by the wee one's.

I struggled to make my feet and Knu clenched harder. It felt like the bones in my forearm were grinding together.

"Don't make me bind you."

I grumbled and moped, glaring at the Sidhe advance and the Judge.

He jumped off his horse, and stripped the skins from his shoulders. He shed the plates guarding his shins and arms, dropped the round wooden shield from his back as he walked toward Shannon.

The Wee Ones were an arm's length apart, and though I couldn't see the symbols and lines etched in the dirt around them, I could feel the waves of power radiating from their position.

"The leprechaun and gnome are an ancient power," Knu recited beside me, lecturing even as we watched destruction approach like a tide. "Their magic is the magic of the creation of all the Universes, manifested in the building of life. As such, it is the power of the gods."

"In a little bitty vessel," I quipped.

She squeezed tighter.

I whined a little bit to let her know it hurt.

"What are they tapping into? The Leyline in Scotland?"

"That and beyond," she said. "There are nexus, crossroads

where the lines intersect not just here, but in multiple universes. These aren't just fonts of power, they are also where the veil is the thinnest."

She looked at me as she said this.

I figured she was imparting something important, so I tried to forget about fighting and focus on what she was telling me.

"Nexus. Doorways. Power. Got it."

She nodded and made me look at the Judge.

He got close to Shannon, only wearing his kilt again.

"He can't break the circle," I whispered.

"Some magic is stronger than the unbroken line," Knu answered.

The Judge reached through the circle around the leprechaun. The field shimmered as his arm slid through. He hesitated for just a moment, just one second, and I saw his face.

He was crying.

Fat swollen tears rolled down his cheeks and trembled on his quivering lips.

The Judge grabbed Shannon and yanked him back through the circle. He threw him across the flat stone, yanked out a knife and slit the Wee One's throat.

Radar cried out as blood leaked from his compatriot.

The Judge moved faster than I had even seen anyone move, an athletic grace that belonged anywhere other than the battle-field.

He reached out, yanked Radar through his circle and slit his throat on top of his friend's.

The small circles collapsed, sending a wave of energy into the larger circle that contained all three. The blood funneled off the stone, it hit a shallow groove carved in the earth, filling the outer circle.

The Judge threw back his head and screamed on top of the glowing corpses of the Leprechauns. A column of blue lightning arced out of the Leyline, sheathing his body in electric light.

I had to turn my head to shield my eyes and saw Knu staring in wonder and horror, tears leaking from her eyes as well.

The light winked out, and I blinked away the after effects strobing purple in my view.

The Judge stood up, astride the bodies on the stone and where he pointed, Sidhe died.

He pushed back the onslaught of attackers, laying waste like a farmer with a sythe slicing down wheat.

The Sidhe on unicorns turned and bolted for the rent in the fabric of our universe.

Only one lived to escape, sacrificing his mount to the magic and crawling through.

I don't know who sealed the rip.

It could have been the Sidhe, to prevent the Judge from sending magic back into their realm. It might have been the Judge to stop any from coming through.

But the black hole disappeared and then it was just clean up. Scratch that.

The Judge did more than clean up.

The blood on the field filled trenches, and I could see another ritual being build.

The battlefield was a giant sacrificial ritual on top of a leyline.

Much like the one I had busted up that brought demons into the world.

I glared at Knu.

"To gain power to fight the enemy, your Judge made a sacrifice."

She said it in a low soft voice that I heard more in my head than with my ears.

I looked back at the man who became something more, something akin to a god and wondered at the mentality it would take to do something like that.

To have so many die at my hands or at my command.

The blood leaking from bodies kept flowing into the trenches, the magic drawing it in like a vacuum.

It was a mixture of life essence, and will power and force of spirit, all trapped, all drawn in and all being channeled, transferred into the Judge.

"He stole their life," I growled.

Thinking again magic thoughts of destruction and ramping up to take on the Judge.

"Memories," Knu reminded me. "He took their magic but he did not steal it."

She lifted us up higher, taller than the trees so I could make out the symbols etched into the dark soil, rent into the rock.

The symbols were of sacrifice, yes.

But of willing sacrifice. For glory and honor, not of battle, but of living.

Tens of thousands of men lined up to fight for the Judge and die for him.

And I could see the symbols under the Wee One's circles.

"Willing," she confirmed. "The sole reason they came."

The Fae sent their own to die, give power to a human and aid him in his fight against the Sidhe.

The light went out, but I wanted to see more.

"I can show you no more," she said. "It's a need to know."

She was one of the ancients, her magic of a kind gifted to a man to fight for them.

But when it came to will power, I'm as stubborn as a mule in a sugar bowl.

One sweet ass.

I set my will against hers, and she laughed.

"Think this is one you can win?"

I set it harder and heard her smirk harder still.

"Here, hold my beer." She joked.

Then she pulled back the curtain of her mind and I started crying. Probably came close to pissing myself.

I'm sure it was like being in the presence of a god, so much power, so much essence, so much of it all.

Life. Will. Freedom. Magic.

She pulled it back before it killed me.

The scene winked back on, and I could see the Judge sitting on the edge of the stone, weeping.

We popped up on the edge of the clearing, outside of the tree line and he looked up, looked in our direction.

I almost spoke, but she held a finger against my lips.

Those blue eyes glared for a moment, searching for us, for the spirits Radar had notices. I could see the red rimmed puffiness, and the sadness destined to become permanent.

He was the last thing alive in this field, and I knew his was the greatest sacrifice for he killed everything he loved and gave up his soul to keep this world safe.

26

CHAPTER TWENTY SIX

Knu snapped her fingers and brought us back to the table by the river. A couple of thousand years and a couple of hundred days in the past, but only a few moments had passed her.

Folks, that's relativity at its finest, which tells you pretty much all you need to know about magic.

It can do.

Whatever.

I let go of the Gnome's hands and wiped my head. The thing about relativity is most of the world we live in is made up of memories. Think about this for a moment, but the reality I was in existed of a park by the river, still warm cup of coffee clutched in my trembling hands.

But that was only what I could see.

I knew the rest of the world still went on around me.

Hannah was at her house, reading and researching. The

witches were out witching, the vampires twitching in their graves. The monsters were doing what demon monsters do when they hide out from sunlight after breaking into this plane.

The Normanii were stalking toward me across the park.

I had faith that the rest of the world went on out of sight and unassisted by me outside my little bubble.

I had memories of what went on out there, like knowing the water sliding past in front of me was in Memphis three days ago. But I didn't have to see it to know it.

Watching the Judge was like that.

It was also like peeking in on parents in the bedroom, I suspect. A weird guilty fascination with what you might see.

I'd seen the Judge.

Perhaps at his worst.

I'd seen the sacrifice he had been willing to make, he had been prepared to give in to, and know how it affected him in the future.

Or at least I thought I did.

Was that past what made him who he was today?

The most powerful wizard to exist.

Or did he do more dastardly things in the interim before I met him and went to work with him? Did he have to keep up the blood sacrifices to maintain his position?

Was he like one of the gods of old, demanding an alter and a sheep every couple of days?

The thought made my head spin.

"Look out," Knu said and ducked.

I didn't.

A punch sent me spinning off the table and I threw up a shield to stop two more.

"You didn't see that coming?" I yelled at her.

"They decided once they got here."

We flicked a spell at the same time, which froze the red faced Northmen in their tracks. There were three of them, Eric I knew, and two others who looked like they belonged on the set of some hot guy calendar shoot.

Seriously, what did these Vikings eat to have such low body-fat? I was tempted to be jealous, but decided to be pissed first.

My sore jaw dictated it.

I stood up and rubbed away some of the sting.

"What about you?" I snarled at the ghost.

"They snuck up on me."

He tried to look innocent.

"Did you want me to take a punch?"

Maybe the ghost was blaming me for getting him killed and now losing his memories. Scratch that, it was my fault Elvis died, so there was no one else to blame.

"Did I want you to? Not until I saw him swinging. Did it hurt?"

"Don't sound so happy about it."

I sat on the bench next to Knu and snapped my fingers to release the men from the spell. The largest one tumbled to the ground, mid-kick, but the others recovered quickly and turned in my direction.

"Let's see how long you can last without a sucker punch," I threatened.

Eric held his hand in front of his warrior buddy to keep him from charging.

"You informed the enemy of our presence and intent," he growled.

Whoa. Angry Viking sounds like a wolf when they're pissed. Good to note.

"I told you in the truck I met a guy on the train," I kept both hands on the table.

Not so they could see them, so I could have a clear shot if they decided to rush me, or whip out swords or do something equally stupid.

"I ran into him again last night and gave fair warning to get out of town."

"He is their Elder," Eric shouted. "He sues for peace now."

The largest Viking spit on the ground in disgust.

"There is no peace with the undead," Eric continued. "But the vampires have sent an emissary to the Jarls."

Knu took a breath beside me, but didn't say anything.

"And you're blaming me?"

"They are a scourge," the giant spit again. "Your interference has halted our mission to destroy them."

I stood up from the table.

They were smart enough to step back.

Well, Eric and the other normal sized guy were, but the tall one looked like he was itching to take a run at me.

I guess he figured brute strength and his size were a match for my speed of thought.

I melted the ground under his feet so he slipped down to his knees, then locked it tight as concrete, just to give him a little reminder that he was dealing with forces beyond his kin.

"Damn it man," he spit again. "These are new boots!"

Not worried about being stuck in the ground. Worried about the leather.

I shook my head.

"I'm sorry I ruined your kill vampire party," I told Eric. "But if the vamps want peace, and your Jarl agrees, then the killing stops."

Eric shook his head.

"No, it does not," I could see the berserker raging inside his eyes, the red glow outlining the iris. "The blood suckers will still prey on the weak. Only they will do so under the aegis of a brokered peace. It will not save humans. It will only be an advantage to the vampires."

"You are responsible for the deaths of a million innocents," the tall one said from his spot in the earth. "What happens from here forward will be on your head. Until I take it."

Let's face it, I kind of liked the guy. Any bad ass who can mouth off threats when you literally have them locked down up to their knees in dirt is someone you want on your side in a fight.

"I like your moxie," I told him and loosened the earth so he could climb out.

He did and sat opposite of Knu to knock the soil from his soles.

"I don't know what I can do," I told Eric. "But I'll hunt up the vampire and see if I can say something. Meet me at the Watcher's house at ten."

"What will you say? What can you say that will stop this?

"I don't know," I figured honesty was the best policy here because even I didn't know how to spin a lie to make it right. "But he seems to respect me. And he's looking out for his people."

"I don't respect that," Eric sneered. "Not at the expense of my people."

Made sense to me.

"I don't respect you," the big guy stomped his feet on the concrete. "A smart man would have thought this through."

I couldn't argue with him there either.

"Next time, try using your words. Less punching the Marshal, more asking politely. Dig?"

"Next time, I will be the one hitting," the big git stood up and towered over everyone.

I turned the dirt under their feet into slushy sand just to let them know I didn't think anyone should be hitting anyone right now, and watched them fumble stumble their way toward the parking lot.

"A little warning next time?" I turned to Knu.

"Like I said, it was a last minute decision. They did come to talk at first."

I nodded.

Murky waters and ripples.

"I need to think about what you showed me."

She sighed.

It must be tough working with children.

"You have no idea," she said. "But there will be food before your meeting tonight."

I didn't ask how she knew about that. Probably picked the details out of my gray matter.

"Happy Hour," she said and named a place. "On me."

Despite the punch, I felt the day improving, as only one about to get free food and drinks coming.

But first, there was work to do to get ready.

For after.

27

CHAPTER TWENTY SEVEN

Vampires don't go out in the sun much and it's not because they shine bright like a diamond or some Pope in the sixteenth century cursed them for day walking.

Turns out, it's just uncomfortable.

Sure, give a vamp enough time and they learn to live with the ache, much as senior citizens learn to live with the dull throb of arthritis, or pretty much anyone learns to deal with backpain.

It hurts. A lot, but eventually, you live with it.

The sun hurts vampires.

No one knows why.

Maybe some scientists did some experiments on it in the Nevada desert and created a race of super vamps resistant to the sun, but newbies hurt the most, and as they move past a couple hundred years, they learn to tolerate it.

As it was, most vamps didn't live past a hundred years.

Or so I'd heard.

Too much infighting, politics and generally bad attitudes that come with too much power too fast.

No sense of responsibility with that lot.

So new vamps preferred the night.

Finding one Elder in a sea of humans that inundated NOLA was nigh on impossible.

But finding a guy who had his fingers in a lot of pies, and a lot of them the illegal kind of pies was a lot simpler.

And a guy with his fingers in so many alleged pies would also know about paranormal activity in his town, since his sun was betrothed to a witch, or beholden to one.

Either way, there was an alliance in the making and I knew the guy trying to pull the strings.

I just had to find him.

There are eyes and ears of a city, a network of spies so observant had Washington used them in the American Revolution it would have been over in less than a year.

You just have to learn to ignore the stench.

I saw a homeless guy sitting on the sidewalk with a battered cardboard sign saying he would work for food.

I got some information from him for ten dollars, and caught a trolley to where he directed.

A dry cleaner's.

A bell over the door tinkled when I pushed through. A smiling Asian man looked up from behind the counter, made a small mouse like squeak and disappeared into the back between racks of floating shirts, suits and what looked to be an Elvis jumpsuit.

"You know what that's about?" I asked over my shoulder.

"I think you scared him."

"I meant the threads."

He floated over and tried to finger the material through the plastic covering, but his wispy hands couldn't grab the fabric.

"Nice workmanship," he stuck his head through the hanging suit.

Another suit walked out from the back, flanked by two large walking slabs of masculinity.

"Digby's dad?" I guessed.

It was an educated guess though, because Daddy Richmond looked like an older, more worn version of the younger.

The man extended his hand, but one of the giants reached out and pulled his hand down. It was like grabbing a snake, and the guy looked just as scared to do it, especially once I saw the look he got for it.

I marked him as the bravest man on earth at that moment.

"He knows what he's doing," I tried to help.

Digby's dad dropped the glare and replaced it with a smile.

"You're right, of course," he snarled and took a moment to compose himself. "I don't like being touched."

"Must make it hard to get that haircut."

Elvis chortled, which made me smile.

Daddy Richmond didn't like being made fun of.

"You're a guest in my town, Marshal. Guests should not make a habit of pissing off their host."

I figured I could play this two ways.

Have a pissing contest with the Dixie Mafia boss and make getting the information I needed twice, maybe three times as hard. Or play nice.

"No need to be so sensitive," I said. "I'm just here to find someone."

"I didn't say you were a welcome guest."

The smile slipped off his face. Heckle and Jeckle stuck their massive hands under their massive coats, no doubt putting them on the butts of massive pistols.

It could have been a big problem.

Marshals are supposed to practice restraint when it comes to the use of magic on mortals.

Turns out that's one of the easiest ways to get a sorcerer label slapped on your reputation, and is a huge part of my job. Hunting down wizards and witches who turn their magic on non-magic users for personal gain.

Never pretty.

I could have ensorcelled the mob boss' mind and made him do my bidding. I had the latitude to do it.

And I was in a hurry.

But the thing about using magic like that is just how slippery the slope can get. When you put your toe over the line into the gray, how far can you go before it gets black?

It's not like there is a highly demarcated DMZ or a guide that lets you know just how far too far is when you start playing around with it.

I thought perhaps it was done in layers.

First, you steal bread to feed your family.

Then, it's just a short hop over to stealing money to buy bread to feed your family, with a bunch of micro-decisions in between, all leading to black magic.

Instead of controlling their minds, I wiggled my fingers and froze his bodyguards.

"I do not wish for things to go badly between us Marshal but if we continue along this path I fear we must."

The man with the moussed up hair stood between his two frozen statues.

He was the type of man who didn't speak in contractions, the type of person who watched old movies to adopt old ways, a southern gentleman, or the portrait of one.

He captured the nuances of charm, but not the essence. It was as fake as the product he wore in his hair, the manicured smile and–

"Are you wearing make up?"

The glare was stronger this time, and I for one, was glad the man wasn't a wizard. That look meant he would have started blasting. As it was, I almost got a sunburn from the color popping up on his cheeks.

"This is that path Marshal."

He was right.

Things could and would go badly between us. There was no way around it and I wasn't looking for one. This petty man with petty dreams hurt people to make his life better.

I wasn't going to stand for it.

Then Digby walked in behind me.

"Hey, it's you!"

He clapped me on the back and stood off to the side from his dad, beaming like he just met an old friend from the frat, in town for a weekend of drinking and football.

I held back the spell and tried to breath.

"Daddy," he said. "This is the man I was telling you about."

Two things.

I know Digby knew what his dad was up to regarding the criminal element. There was just no way around it, and the man was participating in an alliance ritual.

Something was up, I just wasn't sure if this was my problem, or one of those sort it out later problems.

Second, what grown man calls his father daddy?

"We are becoming acquainted," Daddy Richmond answered

in an even voice.

"That's good stuff Daddy," he beamed some more. "I like this one better than the other Marshal. That guy was kind of a dick."

He aimed the last sentence at me, like we were in on a secret.

"We all have that problem sometime," I told him.

Fingers hooked on my belt, thought cocked and loaded.

"What brings you to my establishment, Marshal?" Daddy Richmond asked.

Right. Vampires. And witches. And a demon monster.

"Am I right in assuming you know the comings and goings going on in your town?"

He nodded.

"Daddy knows everything," Digby bragged. "We've got this network of-"

"Digby!" Daddy didn't want him sharing any secrets. "Were you able to speak with the girl?"

The young man nodded, his hair not moving. They must have used the same stylist.

"She's still gung ho."

"Excellent. Marshal, I have other business to which I should be attending. If we could speed this along."

"Vampire convention."

Two words. It was all I needed to say.

Both men blanched. Even the statue guards may have flinched a little bit.

"Conclave," Daddy Richmond said with a shiver.

He knew. Probably one of the blood suckers paid a visit, and offered a tribute. For a mafia man to be afraid of the mere mention of them said the conclave was a dangerous big deal.

"Conclave," I sneered. "Claude?"

"What would you like with him?"

"Magic business," I told him.

The thing about powerful men, especially those who have risen to power through will and hard work, and probably creating ghosts along the way, is they believe in the art of intimidation.

Some try it with a look. Tall guys will use their size. Small guys will use goons with guns.

Daddy Richmond was a looker.

Not a good looking man, though he was that in a Southern gentleman's traditional sense.

But a man who liked to enter stare contests and beat you down with his pupils.

He tried one on for size with me.

It didn't work.

Once you've fought Trolls, and Sidhe and boggarts, some little man in a big town on the Gulf Coast doesn't stand a chance.

Digby watched as his old man looked away, and I saw a tinge of something on the younger's face.

That contest cost Daddy a little more than his pride.

I wouldn't have minded staying around to watch how it played out, but he answered my question with an address.

"But they won't be there until dark," he said.

I nodded and looked over his shoulder at my ghost partner still floating beside the plastic covered jumpsuit.

"Got that?"

"I can remember an address," he sighed.

Digby and Daddy both jumped a little, not at the sound of Elvis' voice, which they couldn't hear, but at the sight of a man just speaking to thin air.

Always leave them wondering if you're crazy, and they would

be insane to mess with you.
So I did.

28

CHAPTER TWENTY EIGHT

Daddy Richmond told me to wait until dark, but I figured that was just to buy some time for Claude to vamoose.

Or set up an ambush.

The thrall answered the door and tried to slam it in my face.

A door to door salesman told me once to always slip your foot against the frame and lean in whenever someone opens the door for the rare occasion they tried to slam it shut.

He had a permanent limp.

But his advice served me well as the door raced for the frame in front of my face.

I didn't need to sacrifice toes to the sales gods though.

I flicked a finger and the solid oak slab with intricate carvings and a brass metal knocker shot back hit with a hurricane blast of force.

The thrall went flying.

The door thudded against the inside wall and planted the wrought iron knob into the plaster lathing.

I had to make another wave to pass through the wards and step inside the hallway.

An inhuman shriek filled the air as death descended the staircase.

Seriously, if you've never seen a vampire in flight, it is a thing of wonder. Of course, most blood suckers are so fast, or people are so hypnotized by them, they would fail to notice the beauty in the descent.

But it is a sight to behold.

I beheld it for about one second and stepped to one side as Claude smashed into the tile floor in a clatter of masonry and stone and whipped around, fangs extended, clawed hands swiping for my oh so tender throat.

Til he hit my shields.

No flying sparks, no nail on chalkboard sound, just a solid thunk where the meat of his flesh met the meat of my magic.

He stopped then and stood up straight from the hunched over more animalistic version of himself.

"Marshal," he bowed his head. "Welcome to my home."

No need to mention the attack or the way I barged in.

No need to discuss how he could have taken my head off if I wasn't magic, or how I could have blasted him mid-air and showered in a confetti of vampire bits.

Just a couple of guys standing in the hall of a nice house on a side street in the French Quarter.

"Nice place," I told him.

"We rented for a month," he reached down and helped the thrall up, brushing off his shoulders and helping to straighten his shirt.

"And thank you for not hurting Thomas."

He ran a loving hand across the head of the shorter man standing next to him. The stoner look was still there, gazing up at Claude in ecstatic rapture.

"You're not going to get your deposit back."

Claude glanced over his shoulder at the damage to the wall and down at his feet.

"Thomas," he said.

The thrall hurried to shut the door, then examined the wall.

"You will find he is quite skilled at many things, home repair one of them. He was a contractor for the clean up."

"He must have appreciated the house he saw this morning," I stared at the vampire.

"He mentioned it. Quality craftsmanship never escapes his eye. He informed me he delivered my message this morning, so imagine my surprise to see you here today and not at our designated meeting place."

"I decided to start the party early."

"I am all for parties," Claude said and invited me to enter further into his lair.

I declined.

"The address on the card?"

"It is the witch which you seek."

"You think that's clever Lestat?"

"I like wordplay as much as playing with my potential supplicants," he smiled.

The fangs were still there.

"The Normanii paid me a visit today."

The fangs extended and the smile turned into something that belonged to a shark.

"Shall we invite them too?"

CHAPTER TWENTY EIGHT

He was kidding. Partially.

The Vikings could do a ton of damage to any collection of vamps and he knew it. Which let me know Claude was up to something.

I just didn't have time to figure out what right now because I had a few more stops to make.

29

CHAPTER TWENTY NINE

I met Knu outside of a pub set up next to the Mississippi River and we had the deck on the second floor all to ourselves before the crowd showed up.

"You know things," I pleaded with the gnome. "We're friends. I helped you."

"I cannot," she said.

Her voice sounded sad, pitiful and small.

I didn't give a damn.

"You know where she is!" I shouted. "Tell me."

"I will not," she said, still sad, still tiny.

I wanted to reach out and make her.

I could. I was strong enough. My fingers twitched with the hint of magic, ready to lift her up and press her against the wall.

Marshal's had to be fast on the draw if they wanted to survive and I'd outlasted almost all of them.

154

Dumb luck mostly.

But enough skill to make it look good.

I pointed and started an incantation.

One word. That's all I had to get out. The Judge made us memorize spells until we could use them without talking, without wands, without anything but the power of our will and minds.

I thought about all of this as I was slammed into the wall upside down and held there by the gnome's magic.

Her fingers didn't move either.

"Are you done?" she said.

Still sad. Sad she couldn't answer me, sad she had to swat me around a little.

"No," I grunted. "You could have let me get something out, just to make me feel better."

She nodded.

"I couldn't take the chance you might hurt me. On accident," she added.

She was a couple of thousand years old, which put her high up on the power totem pole. My spell might have tickled, if she let it get through.

"No," she corrected me. "The Judge chose you for a reason. That reason is your power."

"I'm not that strong," I waved at my boots, which were currently aimed at the ceiling. "Current situation as a prime example."

"It's not just your strength," she twirled her finger and spun me right side up. "It's your will. There are few with more willpower than you."

I adjusted my coat and smoothed back my hair after she settled me on the ground. My little temper tantrum had subsided and I felt a twinge of guilt for trying to force her to talk. Just a little twinge though.

"I'm sorry."

"I know. I could read it up here," she tapped her temple. "I would tell you what you want to know if I thought it would help. But there is the type of knowledge that destroys. This is that."

I sighed.

"Is she alive?"

"Would that make you feel better about the task before you?"

"Hell yeah," I said.

She sniffled and a tiny tear trickled from the corner of her eye.

"It would save you so much pain if you could just accept that she was dead."

The way she said it.

"She's not?"

The gnome shook her head.

"The woman who was your wife still lives."

"There's nothing cryptic about that statement at all," I said.

"I can say no more. You wished to know if she was alive. She is. But she is not who she was."

I took a deep breath and let a long sigh leak out of my nose.

"It's future stuff," she told me. "Right now, there's a witch to find in NOLA."

I took another breath, and this time held it.

She was right. I asked to know, and she told me.

I wanted more, but this would have to be enough for now.

I turned some bad mojo loose on the world and the Judge tasked me with cleaning it up.

There was also a vampire convention going on, and I needed to check in on that power struggle too.

And think about everything I had learned in our visit to the past, because I felt like there were some answers in there too.

Oh yeah, and help Elvis keep his memory, and move on to a better place.

Damn, my list was getting longer.

"It will get longer still," she said reading my head.

I grinned.

"I didn't stand a chance at getting the draw on you, did I?"

She smiled.

"You surprised me in the park. It is possible. Not likely, but always possible."

I nodded.

I'd have to be content with that.

Right now, there was witch hunting to be done.

Right after happy hour.

"Seven billion humans," she said and sipped her drink.

There was an empty glass waiting for the waitress to pick it up and the gnome was halfway through the second.

I didn't feel so bad about my craft beer.

"They're killing us, you know. Killing magic."

I wanted to argue, wanted to say I was human and that it wasn't true.

Except it was. We were.

"Each of those billions have an effect on their environment," the gnome slurred.

"They touch on the, what do you call it? Quantum level. The atoms and things that make up this world and others."

That made sense to me. Seven billion actions by people every second of every day was bound to create ripples, changes.

"We argued for killing you off," she confided in me. "All of you. Back before you spread across the land like a plague."

"In some places, we succeeded," she ticked them off on her fingers. "Cro-magnum, the pygmy races, Bigfoot, the missing link. Each branch of the evolutionary tree, save one. You. Homo-Sapiens. Pets for the vampires."

"I didn't know that," I told her.

"Not many do. Something about your blood, the way it tastes."

She finished her drink, and made a circle finger motion that could have been interpreted as one more round or bring the check.

I put a hand on my wallet to pick up the tab, but the waitress showed up with a refill for her and a fresh bottle for me.

I wasn't going to complain.

"The vamps liked you around for fodder. But the fodder got loose cause some gods liked playing with you and the next thing you know, here we are. Seven billion reasons the planet is dying, magic is dying."

She pulled on the straw to wash away the thought and stared at me with bleary eyes.

"Do you know how hard it is to see the future in the first place," she asked.

I shook my head.

"Must be tough," I sympathized.

"Let me tell you how tough," she put a friendly hand on my forearm and leaned in to tell me her secrets.

"See the river? See how muddy it is?"

I nodded.

"Could you find a school of fish in that water? Could you pick out one particular fish out of all the ones living and moving in that river?"

I shook my head no. It did sound too tough.

"It's like that," she winked. Trying to determine if the ripples and Eddie's are the one fish you want to find and follow."

She leaned back then for another sip.

"Now multiply it by years, by millions of people who've traipsed across the paths you must go, and where you have been. It is almost impossible."

Her eyes grew serious and sober.

"But for magic. That's what makes it work for my kind. Faith that it will be. No try. Just do."

She sounded a lot like a little green fellow I liked from the movies, and a mantra for my own line of tough work.

She smirked.

"Who do you think they based it on? One of us."

So, she was a mind reader too.

"Not exactly," she corrected me out loud. "You wear your thoughts on your face. That is perhaps why the Judge values you so much."

I didn't think so.

I mean, I was good at what I did, but that was farm boy training that stuck with me for ninety years. There is a job to be done. Just saddle up and do it.

"I don't think he likes me one way or the other," I told her.

The Gnome's serious eyes grew sad and she blinked back tears as she stared at me.

"Poor fish," she reached out and held my forearm again. "If you only knew what lies ahead."

I didn't get the chance to ask.

One of those ripples in the current of life, or maybe it was an eddy that blocked her view stopped her from talking. She gaped at the figure who stepped through the door. I used the mirror behind her to watch and I gaped too.

No matter what the gnome planned to tell me, neither one of us expected this.

Gloria of the Memphis witches pulled a scarf off her head and made a beeline for our seats.

30

CHAPTER THIRTY

"Fancy a boy like you in a place like this," she pulled out a chair and sat across from us at the table.

"Do you know how hard you are to find?"

I almost spelled her.

Marshals train. A lot. The Judge makes sure we're the fastest guys and gals in the room no matter who we come up against.

To do that, we forgo wands and pointing and any of the other signals that would tell our opponent to get ready, bad stuff is coming down the pipe.

No, the Judge trains us to use our mind and only our mind to cast.

It ain't easy.

And the woman across from me seemed to know that.

She motioned for the waitress by calling out across the bar, ensuring every head in the room turned to look at her.

Sure, I could have popped her head off, or popped her heart, or gave her a raging case of genital warts but the problem was people were watching.

About fifty of those seven billion souls the gnome had just been bitching about were in for some happy hour libation.

I didn't want to give them a story to tell and I saw a couple of phones out and up, ensuring any sort of action had the potential to end up being live streamed.

"Nice company you keep," she slathered on a smile that looked sincere. "Am I interrupting a first date."

"Sidhe," the Gnome spat and did something with her fingers.

A protective spell popped up around her as Gloria the good witch made finger motions back, sending little sheets of sparks to bounce off the gnomes up stretched hand.

"There's no smoking in here," the waitress sneered.

She must have mistaken the light show for lighters

"You can get cancer on the deck though."

I snorted.

She must have cared more about her lungs than a tip, but I can't say I blamed her. I came of age when doctors were prescribing cigarettes as cures and taking massive payoffs from the tobacco industry to do it.

I guess they still did, only now it was with opium instead of leaves.

"What can I get you?" she asked Gloria.

"Out of here, "I advised.

"Dirty martini," the Witch ignored me.

I decided to press for some info if she was planning to stay.

"Why did she call you Sidhe?"

Gloria laughed.

"Takes one to know one," her voice tinkled.

"It is possessed," the Gnome spat from behind her protective shield.

"Possessed?"

"She looks human," I said confused.

"Oh Darling, that's the whole idea."

I froze with my bottle halfway to my lips. My brain wouldn't work, I was vapor locked by one word she let slip from those luscious lips.

Darling.

"I'm so sorry," the Gnome glanced at me. "I would have told you had I known."

Only my wife called me darling. Just like that.

Same tone. Lilt to the voice, tilt to the head

I couldn't move.

Couldn't breathe.

"Son of a bitch," Elvis said it for me.

The spell slipped, just a bit.

And I saw her.

The face was different, distorted by the possession that changed everything about her. Look, smell, touch, feel. Even her mind was different as I reached out and probed with magic. But the essence was there, a hint of her soul.

And it had changed.

I looked at the Gnome, at tears streaming down her wrinkled cheeks. She looked heartbroken, and then I realized it was pity.

At me.

"How?" I stuttered.

Gloria laughed again as the waitress set a dirty martini in front of her. She pulled out a man's wallet and passed the girl a crisp one hundred dollars bill.

"These don't stop until I say they do. And one more round

before they're cut off."

The girl smiled and scampered off after tucking the bill in her pocket.

"How?" Gloria took a drink and smacked her lips. She fished out an olive and popped it in her mouth. "Tell him."

"A Sidhe only takes over by invitation," the Gnome grimaced. "It is a union that cannot be broken."

I watched her fingers twitch as she tried to scry the next few moments, few hours. She was looking for my reaction, and the actions that would have strong repercussions.

"Why would I want to break it?" Gloria trilled. "Your wife gave up her body in exchange for power. Neither of us would wish it back."

I took a breath to cast.

I was gonna destroy it and damn the consequences. I'd kill every last person in the bar if I had to.

The Gnome clutched my arm, sharp nails digging in and stopping me.

"The Judge looked for you," I said.

Even to me it sounded desperate. It would have been better if I casted and damn the consequences.

"That old fool," Gloria snorted. "He found me. Guess he didn't want you to know."

The room started spinning and I could hear the blood pumping in my ears. It sounded like the shuffling of a bull about to charge.

"Here you go," said the waitress depositing another beer in front of me and a glass in front of the gnome.

I reached out, lifted it to my lips and drained the bottle.

"What do you want?"

She smiled and I could see it in her features. The Sidhe

had changed the shape of her face, but it was like looking at someone who got plastic surgery. There was a hint of her sister in there, and I was going to need to contact her.

I suspected she was a Valkyrie and wondered if that was why the Sidhe targeted her.

What would her sister do?

I set the beer down on the table, careful of my shaking hands. Spells whirled in my head, twirled around in a vortex of rage and pain, a hurricane of emotion that needed an outlet.

"I want you to go home," she said. "I'll even meet you there once this is all done."

"What is this?" I asked.

I couldn't let go of the beer bottle. The thick brown glass creaked and shifted under my palm. Knu put her hand on my forearm again, trying to center me, trying to keep me from reacting.

"This is a mess you created when you interfered," Gloria said.

Her auburn hair was so different from the blond I knew. Hey eyes slightly canted up in the corners. I could see the person who had been my wife, but I could also note the influence of the Sidhe possessing her.

"Stopping you," I muttered.

It came out a little pettier than I intended and she remarked upon it.

"Petty doesn't become you."

"If I was that dress I'd be coming on you too," I snapped.

The bottle shattered in my fist, sharp pain lancing through the skin of my palm as shards ripped it apart. The beer burned in the cuts and the waitress shouted from across the room.

"I'll bring you a rag to clean up!"

She didn't notice the blood.

The Sidhe did.

Gloria licked her lips.

"What a waste," she purred and reached out a finger to steal some of the crimson life on the table.

"Nein!" Knu crackled a force shield over the bloodstain on the table.

Protecting me from who knew what kinds of horror a magic creature beyond the veil could do with the blood. Keeping me safe from the woman I loved, the woman I missed for the past decade. The woman I would now have to mourn.

Gloria drew back her finger like touching an electric outlet and cursed in a language that hadn't been heard on earth in ten thousand years or longer.

Or it could have been Latin, I needed to brush up.

"Ix-nay on the touching my od-blay," I wiggled a finger in the air, making sure Gloria could see the tip of the long digit.

She might be natural magic contained in a human vessel, an immortal creature who maybe even created the quantum rules by which magic exists, but I was a damn Marshal.

And no matter what deal my wife made to let this thing use her body it wasn't going to get a piece of mine.

Not without a fight.

Gloria laughed.

"I have her memories of you in here," she sneered. "And I remember the way you fumbled in Memphis. You're a child."

Her eyes turned to Knu.

"Both of you, children. Your limited minds couldn't comprehend the depth of my abilities. That is why she surrendered to me. The power. The exchange was... glorious."

The waitress hustled over with a bar towel.

"You're bleeding," she gagged and feinted.

I spun out of my seat and caught her with my good hand before she cracked her head on the tile, but that gave Gloria a chance to hop away from the table. She backed toward the door.

"Go home Marshal. Your Judge has set you on an impossible task and you are in over your head. You're just going to get more people killed."

"Shoot her," Elvis shouted.

"I'm going to save her," I said to Gloria.

Gloria stopped and beamed in ecstasy.

"You don't know!" she crowed and did a tiny jig with her feet. "She can't be saved Marshal. Your wife gave up her very soul when she invited me in. She is gone. Forever."

I shot a thought at her face then.

It couldn't be helped.

Gloria snapped up a hand and batted it away, laughing as she slipped through the door.

The manager arrived at the same time as Knu, taking over care for the fallen waitress who was moaning as she came around.

I stood up, dripped blood on the floor next to her and she passed out again. She was cared for, so I bolted toward the door and slammed through it with my shoulder.

Gloria was gone.

But the sound of her laughter lingered. I couldn't tell if it was just in my mind or on the wind.

31

CHAPTER THIRTY

"I need some time," I yelled at Knu.

I didn't care if she wanted to hang me up by my heels again, I was pissed.

"I didn't know," she pleaded. "That is something I would have shared."

Maybe she would have.

Maybe not.

But I came to NOLA to do a job, and I was finding out a lot more than I wanted to know.

Like my wife was dead.

I opened my mouth to say something smart, something pithy, something with wit and bite, designed to cut her to the bone and leave her second guessing everything about her life.

It came out as a sob.

Then my eyes watered up and I ran.

It's hard to run in hiking boots, but not impossible. I ran as fast as I could from the bar on the river.

I pounded on the pavement past the park. I crossed traffic, ignoring the honking horns and the swerving cars, the sound of tires screeching on the pavement.

I ran in front of a trolley to beat it, and felt the edge tug against my bomber jacket.

I stopped at a park in the center of town, a memorial to a jazz man and his trumpet and sat under a tree with my face in my hands.

The tears kept coming.

"Marshal?" Elvis said from beside me. "That was a wild run through town but it's time to sober up."

"Not now Elvis," I had to clear my throat to speak.

"Now," the ghost hissed.

I looked up just in time.

"Look who's weeping in fear," the giant Viking sent a kick at my head as he stomped up to the tree.

I ducked aside and he hit the trunk, shaking loose leaves.

"You have the worst timing," I grunted and rolled away.

The earth under his feet turned to slush but he jumped before he sank, grabbed a branch and kipped a kick at my head again.

I ducked back, thought the branch into manacles and let him hang there like a piñata.

"This is going to hurt you a lot more than it hurts me," I warned him and shot a lance of force into his stomach.

Then I had to stand back as he vomited all over the ground at our feet.

"I told you," I said.

I wiggled the branch and he slipped to the ground, too out of it to jump as I dissolved the ground under him and let him slip in up to his head.

Time to solve this problem like a soccer hooligan.

I took four steps back, lined up on an imaginary goal post and got ready to punt his face.

"Bad idea," said Elvis.

"Stow it," I took two steps forward and a monster plowed into me.

I tried to roll and get away from it, but a giant wolf snapped at my face, latched onto my forearm and shook me like a rag doll.

"Cats and Dogs," I cursed.

The Hund yelped and shrank into a cute little Yorkshire terrier. It still ravaged my arm, but the tiny teeth couldn't tear loose from the rips in the leather it had made in a much larger version.

I rolled up to my feet and tried to decide if I was going to shotput the pup, or just put it down to nip my ankles.

"Your back," Elvis said as a second Hund slammed into me.

I rolled with this one too, keeping it from biting and crashed into the trunk of the tree.

At least I had something to lean against as I climbed up again.

"I'm getting pretty damn tired of stuff knocking me down," I raged and sent a circle of force out around me.

It slammed Eric and the other Viking down, plus the two Hunds. The giant and his terrier were unfazed they were so close to the ground.

"Hold Marshal!" Eric yelled as he backflipped to his feet.

I could see his eyes glowing red, the berserker in him ready to come out and play.

I almost invited him.

A good fight with three Vikings and their Hell Hunds would help ease my soul, and if they happened to do some damage along the way, so much the better.

I could deal with physical pain.

It might even take my mind off my heart for a moment.

Elvis put his hand on my shoulder and sent a cold shiver down my spine.

"You've got to cool it down," he sang.

"A boy band?"

He shrugged and I stood up straight, rage leaking off me as reason fought its way back in.

"We are no boy band," Eric said, misunderstanding. "But we fight like one this day."

I turned the earth to muck around the giant and used magic to lift him up. He'd have to bathe himself, but I shot a blast of air across him to clean off most of it.

He looked ready to fight for a second, then threw back his head and howled.

"Did you see what he did to my Hund!"

He bent over and scooped up the terrier to go nose to nose.

"By Odin's beard man, you turned it into a rat!"

He laughed and was joined by the others, even the two Hunds with their tongues hanging out.

The terrier wasn't having it.

It barked and yipped and growled, first at me, then at the rest of the group.

"I can fix it," I let them know as I leaned against the tree.

I tried wiping my arm across my eyes in a discreet way.

The giant didn't care.

"Why were you crying in the garden Warlock?"

"He's not a warlock, Rollo," Eric corrected. "He is the Marshal of Magic and he bested you in battle."

Rollo grinned.

"My apologies Marshal, I meant no disrespect. My tongue often engages before my brain can catch up."

"I had something in my eye," I explained.

"Both eyes," the giant bent his head down to examine my face and made a tsking noise with his lips.

"Those are tears man."

"If he doesn't want to share with us Rollo, that is his prerogative."

The Hund next to Eric padded over and leaned against my leg.

Her fur was golden brown and warm, and she gazed up at me, I could feel her sympathy, and let my hand drift over her head.

"I've never petted a HellHund before."

"Werewolves," said Rollo as he held up the terrier for a more thorough examination. "Do you think if he changed back, he would be a tiny man?"

"Let's not find out," Eric eyed the Hund against my leg with a strange look in his eye.

I formed the thought in my head and wiggled the spell at the tiny little dog.

It yelped, jumped and transformed back into the giant Hund it had been when it attacked me.

Then it plowed into Rollo and knocked him down.

The giant laughed again.

"Guess he didn't like being picked up," he said as he got up and dusted himself off.

"I don't believe in happenstance," I told Eric. "I have an address for you tonight."

He nodded and took down the numbers.

"And I need a favor," I said.

"A good trade?"

"I need you to find a witch."

32

CHAPTER THIRTY

I sent the Normanii on an errand to find Beth and bring her to me. She had information I needed.

It had to be connected and I just needed some quiet time to figure it out. The vampires showing up at the same time as the voo doo witch and the soul monster meant an orchestrated assault.

I'd put it all on the Judge, but he sent me here to stop it. Clean up my own mess as he put it.

Then my own mess showed up.

He had to have known she would be here.

Hell, he probably knew her next move before he did.

The question was why?

Why put the Normanii and me on the same path?

Why put me on the same train as Claude?

And why hide the death of my colleague from me in the middle of a task?

"How many Marshals have I seen die?" I asked my ever-present ghost.

"Seen?"

Too many, I confirmed. I knew it, just wanted to double check. Our job was to go up against some baddies and there were a lot of those on the seven continents.

I'm not sure how the Judge picked us.

With an average life span of eighteen months, it wasn't a lottery anyone wanted to win.

None of that great powered, great responsibility crap. A Marshal trained to fight black magic with even worse magic.

We went after whoever the Judge said to go get, and I was confident that I was one of the few who brought most back alive.

I'd done enough damage in the war that killing was my back up option.

And the disappearance of my wife had made me revere that spark of life a little too much.

What was I going to do now?

She was dead.

Her body possessed by a Sidhe.

And the man I worked for knew but didn't tell me.

I drew circles on the concrete table top with the tip of my finger, and only noticed the heat etched concrete when a wisp of smoke hit my nose.

There were arcane symbols dredged up from my subconscious, circles and swirls and a letter.

"Do you know this?" I asked the ghost.

Elvis floated over and studied the symbol for a moment.

"That is no bueno," he said. "Where did you see it?"

"I didn't know I had," I confessed. "What does it mean?"

His eyes drifted off, vacant as he tried to remember.

"Not now," I muttered. "I need you to remember."

"I'm caught in a trap," he looked at me and sobbed. "I can't walk out."

It's almost broke my heart. My poor friend.

"We know where to look," I told him.

I patted my bomber pocket for a pen and a scrap of paper to scribble the symbol down.

Eric and his Hunds were back in an hour.

It would almost be worth turning a bunch of people into werewolves just so they could hunt down missing persons. And attach them to Viking warriors to mete out Justice when they found those who took them.

Beth did not look happy.

"I'm not happy about this," she seethed.

Most witches need time to set up rituals before they can perform their magic, and recharge their energy.

That's why it takes so much training to control magic, and what most users don't know is there is an eternal battery source in faith in the quantum aspect of magic.

The Judge teaches it, but I had to be careful, because once I learned he transformed from human to wizard with a giant blood sacrifice, it might affect my belief ability.

Better to not think of it, and focus on Beth.

She was still pretty, and being angry just made her more attractive. Pert lips pursed in anger, brown eyes drawn in consternation.

"I thought if the Marshal had business with me, he wouldn't send his lackey's to find me."

"I'm in a hurry," I said and shifted my arm.

"It looks like you're sitting in a park," she snapped and froze. "What is that?"

She pointed at the symbol.

"Do you know it?"

"No," she lied.

"Jenny I've got your number, I need to change your mind," Elvis crooned.

She shivered.

"Are you doing spirit magic?" she growled.

Eric and the Hunds shifted as they searched for spirits.

"No one here but us chickens," Elvis said.

"What does the symbol mean? I've seen it before, but I can't place it."

"Ask your Watcher," she seethed.

"Lady," I shook my head. "I'm tired. I'm hungry. I got a crap ton of bad news today and I just want a beer."

"I don't care about your problems," she said. "I've got problems of my own."

"I know. A fight with a witch named Phyllis."

"How did you know that?"

"The alliance ritual you were doing with Digby. Your coven is weak. You're weak."

"I am not," she said in a soft voice, cowed.

"Alright," I gave her some wiggle room. "You're not weak. You're just tired, and you're building a coven in one of the most highly magicked cities in the world. There's a lot of history here, and I don't have time for a lesson. I'm here to stop a demon, and I think Phyllis has teamed up with it."

Beth chewed on her lip for a few moments.

"I don't have much power, Marshal," she said after a moment. Her eyes flared. "But what I do have, I offer to assist you."

I nodded.

"So, what does the symbol mean?"

"I don't know it's meaning, but I have seen it. It was carved into the skull of my familiar when I brought it back to life."

"Which was yours? The Giant cats or the really giant saber tooth?"

"Saber tooth!" Elvis shrieked. "You said razor!"

His outburst sent a shiver through all of us and set the Hunds to howling.

I waved him down.

"Saber, razor, it's the same thing."

Talking to the air got me some crazy looks.

Looks that said I might be on the crazy side too.

I didn't worry about it. Added to the myth.

"Saber."

I stored that away for a moment. It didn't help me for right now.

"Alright, I said. "Here's the plan."

I outlined what I wanted to happen with the witch and her coven, and she agreed.

"Bring the cats too," I said.

She raised an eyebrow.

"Are you sure?"

"Cats and dogs in the same place," I shrugged. "What could possibly go wrong."

"You're nothing like the other Marshal," she said after studying me for a moment.

"So I'm told."

"He did not have the same...humor as you."

Good word choice. Very careful.

"I've been at it a little longer than him," I said. "Not so much to prove to witches that get out of hand."

She nodded, warning heard.

"We will strive to stay in hand, Marshal."

"Viking," I called to Eric.

"Normanii," he corrected.

"Northman," I said. "Take the witch home, then meet me at that address at ten o'clock. We have to be done in an hour, because I have an appointment at midnight."

Then I took the ghost to the place we could find answers.

33

CHAPTER THIRTY ONE

I knocked on Hannah's door and waited for her to answer. She opened it after a few moments and handed me a bottle of beer.

"Good guess," I said and took a sip as I stepped in.

She held a twin bottle up to clink against mine.

"What do they say about great minds?" She grinned. "They're dirty as hell."

We toasted and I settled on the couch as she curled up in the chair.

"Any word?" We both asked at the same time.

I was hoping the Judge would send back up, but no such luck.

She shook her head and sipped her beer.

"Here's what we have," I told her and pulled out the paper from my jacket pocket.

"Dog into this and see if you can find something on this."

"Did you draw this?"

"Not originally, no. It looks Celtics or Norse, so start there."

"I mean is this your handwriting?"

"Yeah, I copied it. Why?"

"It looks like a child did it."

"I was drawing on concrete," I told her. "And I was in a hurry."

"You want me to find kid glyphs?"

"We think it's important."

"Who is we?"

"Me I mean."

She stared at me with crunched up eyebrows.

"Please don't tell me I'm going to get that weird when I get old," she teased. "Talking to myself, making up ancient symbols."

"Comes with the territory," I told her. "And what do you know about ghost lore?"

"I need more than that."

I sat back and took a drink then looked at the label on the bottle.

Another beer from Abita, this one Amber. Darker and stronger. I sighed and relaxed into the question.

"Ghost history, ghost physiology? Anything we can find on ghosts and the process by which they lose memories. Seen anything like that?"

She put the tip of the bottle against her lips and played with it long enough to have me second guessing my decision from the night before.

Then she shook her head.

"I know where to start," she said. "But that might take awhile. Which is priority?"

She held up my chicken scratch drawing, which really I should have done a better job on capturing since it might be the key we needed.

I glanced over my shoulder and sighed.

"Picture," I said.

"That's being generous," she shifted out of the chair and rummaged through a pile of books to start her search.

34

CHAPTER THIRTY TWO

I was never large on leadership in my Army days. I had a strict doctrine of follow orders and only assume command in the absence of competent leadership until such a time as I'm relieved of duty.

It happened once.

I assumed command and they wanted me to keep it with a battlefield promotion.

The Judge had other ideas.

Turns out, he'd been keeping tabs on me since I was a kid and liked my moxie.

He didn't call it that. I'm not sure what they called it when he was a kid, if he ever was one. He might have sprung full grown from the mind of Odin or whatever Celtic god passed for the Far Walker back in his day.

My moxie as he called it was a straight forward direct assault.

With a little samurai wisdom thrown in.

One of the priests at the orphanage I was raised in had spent time in Japan when it was still closed off to Westerners. He'd been ship bound to China when a storm washed them up on the volcanic shores of North Japan and the edge of an epidemic.

He wouldn't talk about it much, but he had experience with magical things, as it turned out, most of the priests in the place did.

And he had taught me some tenets that stuck with me through the years.

One was, if a man is worth threatening, he is worth killing straight away.

Samurai considered threats a waste of breath.

Which is what made me a shoot first kind of guy when the situation called for it.

I balanced that yin with a yang for diplomacy.

I'm not sure how much childhood affects our adult life, habits and way of thinking, since I couldn't remember my parents who were killed when I was very young. But they died in violence, I have been told, and so my penchant to do violence first was a back burner item, a last result of sorts.

I'd rather try to talk it out first.

When that didn't work, it was time for the fireworks, and shoot to kill.

I wanted to find Phyllis and give her a chance to talk.

I could have used the zombie attack as an excuse to blast her to nothing, but I'd rather turn her over to the Judge and let him do the whole thing he was named for doing.

Plus, a black magic woman like her might know something about a soul monster roaming the city, word of which had yet to reach my ears.

I'd found a gang war, a zombie uprising, a vampire convention, but nothing of what I'd been sent to stop.

And the gnome wasn't helping.

What good was a psychic medium if they didn't tell you the path you needed to tread?

There are reasons most folks don't know about magic. Sure they believe it, like children on the edge of ten still sort of believe in Santa Claus and the Easter Bunny, but also know that only babies still believe that stuff.

We grow out of belief.

Most of us.

I didn't have that luxury. I was born to magic parents into a magic time just before world war two. My parents were attacked by the Catholic Church and disappeared, which happens a lot more than you think to folks with the ability. I was put in the care of a priest who led the attack on my parents who raised me in an orphanage under his tutelage.

Seriously I didn't have any hang ups about my parents. My childhood was mostly idyllic or at least as sane as a kid raised in a private boarding school monastery could be.

I had new roommates each year, and one or two close friends and was always under the watchful eye of the Father. I was instructed in the rosary and confession, was denied communion until my confirmation and that wasn't allowed until after I hit puberty. That's when they expected any latent magic to appear.

The first signs came when I was ten.

By the time I was twelve I knew I was different and hid it, like most boys who hide their secret longings in their heart or behind bathroom doors.

My body was changing, and whenever the Father tried to question me about it, I just assumed he was referring to the hair in new places.

For my twelfth birthday, Father tried to kill me.

It didn't take.

I spent the next four years on the run, living on the streets of city to city, traveling the rails like a hobo. I met a bunch of people, some kind, others not. The kind ones got a little luck on their behalf in the form of magic, just whatever favor I could send their way. A farmer fed me more eggs than I could eat, then boiled two dozen for me to carry with me. I put a blessing on his cows and chickens so they produced more milk and eggs that never spoiled and never went bad.

A grandmother made me cookies once and I put a ward on her home so that bad weather and bad things just avoided it.

Two boys were travelling on horseback to New York and shared their meager meal with me one night and I gave them eternal safety, a personal ward that stayed with them for almost eight decades.

I won't share the details of the bad men.

They were mostly men and they are mostly dead. Men who prey on children deserve horrible deaths, and I gave it to them, and watched while it happened.

The first time I felt guilty.

Good old fashioned catholic guilt for taking the life of another. I didn't like it, I didn't like how it made me feel. Except that I knew that with these types of people gone the world would be a better place.

I sometimes think about that in the dark of the night. When I can't sleep and I wonder about the dark side and the light side. The two wolves that fight inside us and the stronger one is the wolf we feed, if you believe in Cherokee legend.

I could have been a really great Dark Wizard. Maybe not a

great wizard, but just great at being bad.

Dark magic is usually used against innocent normal people and done so the magician gains advantage.

When those bad men tried to do worse things to me, I tapped into dark magic to cause them grievous harm. I did unto their person horrors that dwarfed the acts they planned for me.

And when they died I moved on.

Maybe it was the Father's influence that kept me from becoming an evil man.

At sixteen, I joined the War.

It was in the war I learned that the world was a whole hell of a lot bigger than anyone knew, and that we were under constant attack from creatures of legend.

They wanted our world, and they wanted us in it, subjugated to their will and moving to their amusement. The Sidhe.

Creature of fairie and fae, legend lost to modern man and slowly being forgotten much like the magic everyone once believed in. How they hated us, hated that they relied on us to believe in them and that their paths to our world were being severed as we destroyed the wilderness in the name of progress.

The Sidhe kept coming at us and though forbidden by an edict older than even their memory against direct interference they still used their influence to try to usurp control of man.

They wanted us to remember them, and fear them. Fear their magic which we no longer believed in.

They were bad.

It was one of the reasons I said yes when the Judge told me I was a Marshal.

Justice against the bad things.

And I never once considered that I might be one of them.

"They're late," I said staring at the clock on the wall. "Send them after me when they get here."

I slid into my coat, checked to make sure the badge was on my belt, then took off to an address a vampire gave me in the dark.

"I sometimes wonder if I'm a special kind of stupid," I muttered to Elvis.

"I don't wonder at all," he answered floating behind me.

35

CHAPTER THIRTY THREE

The dark streets of New Orleans do not go to sleep around the French Quarter. The denizens of daylight go into their homes, shut the doors and pull the curtains to do the things that people do inside walls after dark.

Dinner. Television. Some light reading. Some love making.

The denizens of the night come out at sunset and create a world all of their own unlike any other.

Vampires roamed the city, nibbling necks of visiting tourists who flashed their boobs for the privilege. Witches plied their trade, sharing the streets with pickpockets, drunks, muggers and even priests who vied against all to save the souls of the party crowd.

The Vampire Conclave was held at a manor home that dated back to the war of 1812. There was no sign on the door, nor a banner on the fence to announce the gathering.

Just silent shadow figures moving with an unworldly grace toward the entrance.

I stared at the address and tried to find the angle.

Going in the front door would be suicide.

I'm good, but I'm not stupid. I'd counted to a hundred figures first, then gave up as even more kept showing up.

Claude had directed me to smaller home next door. It was a classic Cajun structure, newer than the manor by several decades, the bottom floor covered storage and the living space on the second and third floors. A set of wide stairs led up from the cobblestone path to a wraparound porch that circled the entire structure, ceiling fans whirring in the humid night air.

The sound of drunken laughter cut across the open space between the buildings as whatever merriment went on at vampire parties carried out of doors.

I imagined it involved blood.

But none of it innocent.

That would be a violation of the Vampire agreements. They were only allowed to partake of the willing, an agreement they created and enforced of their own volition before the Judge sent in a Marshal to do it for them.

I hadn't had a call to fight the vamps yet.

Besides, the Normanii were doing a good job of culling the herd of predators.

And Claude seemed nice. I would hate to have to kill him.

I counted eighteen steps to the second floor and opened an unlocked door.

It was one huge open space that ran the length of the home, all the windows blacked out with mirror tint that hid the light inside. A fireplace dominated one wall, but there was little in the way of furniture.

All cleared out to make room for six dozen vampires.

This was the real conclave, I gulped.

There was power in this room, thrumming like electrical energy and I fought back a shiver.

Like walking into the lion's den.

I didn't have a tin man with me.

"Every breath you take," Elvis crooned at a whisper. "I'll be watching you."

He was referring to the eyes of the predators locked on me as I stepped through the door and closed it behind me.

I could feel two dozen take my measure, heard them sniff as they caught wind of the warm blood coursing through my veins, and shift closer for inspection.

I slid the jacket aside so anyone could see the badge and took some satisfaction in the change in mood.

No one was very interested in me anymore.

They even parted as I moved toward the other end of the building where the action seemed centered.

I came in for a closer look until the vampires stood shoulder to shoulder like a granite wall, transfixed on what was happening on the other side.

CHAPTER THIRTY FOUR

"Venerated Elder, the voice said in a used car salesman rasp. "Your time has long passed. Welcome to the revolution."

"Who the hell is that guy?" Elvis asked.

"Why don't you float up and see?"

He blew out his lips like the idea had never occurred to him and lifted off the ground. He was back in a moment and looked bemused.

"Some clown with a bad dye job showboating," he said.

Not one to miss a good showboat, I parted the vamps like the Red Sea and got a clear view to the guy talking. They did not like being moved by magic, and I heard mutterings, but no one retaliated.

They were transfixed on the orator strutting around in front of Claude. He was ripped muscles and boiling energy, a peroxide blond with spiky hair and rainbow sunglasses.

He was also standing over a woman. She was spread out on a table like a buffet, tied down so I knew this was no thrall making an offer.

"Hey, dye job," I called out. "Who the hell are you?"

That got a few eyes turned my way. All of them. Except the girl. She had hers screwed shut like she was blocking out a nightmare.

The show boating vamp half turned away from Claude and glared at me with red rimmed eyes.

"You called the Marshal on me?" He sneered. "Weak old man, you can't fight your battles on your own."

Claude glared at everyone, and even I could tell he was still in fighting form. No vamp lived as long as he did without collecting a few fangs.

But showboating requires a certain finesse and the young blonde nosferatu looked skilled at it.

"Tyler," he sneered and bowed as he introduced himself.

"Ty," I said. "I hate to break up the party at the conclave but your guest looks like she would rather be elsewhere."

"Tyler," he growled a correction.

"Isn't that what I said?"

"No," he seethed.

"Pretty sure it is, Ty," I looked around to the other undead for support but they were busy looking anywhere but at me.

Except Claude who was smiling. Like he knew a secret.

And then I noticed they were all watching Tyler.

Waiting.

"I will give you one chance to leave before I destroy you and feast on your bones."

"Whoa, that's pretty specific Ty. Not to mention gross. Would it change your mind if you knew I kicked a Troll's ass yesterday?"

"Day before," Elvis corrected.

"Day before," I adjusted.

I watched him.

Personally, I think if a man is worth threatening, then he is worth killing first. Tyler was making a show for the audience of young vampires gathered.

It would have been smarter for him to attack without warning. As it was he flashed across the room like a vampire bat out of hell ready to rain down some blood sucking vengeance on my person.

Magic at the speed of thought, I took a fistful of force and smacked him like a baseball through the wall.

I was a little disappointed he didn't leave a hole the shape of a person in the opening.

"Homerun!" I called out. "And the crowd goes wild!"

They didn't.

"Marshal," Claude tried to warn me.

Too late.

Ty burst up out of the floor like a stripper out of a cake at a bachelor party. He grabbed my ankle as he passed, flipped me up and banged my noggin off the tile.

Remember that scene in the superhero movie where the big Green giant grabs Loki and smacks him around a little bit.

Like a doll?

It was like that.

And in this scene, the part of the Norse God of mischief was played by me.

Except I couldn't even whimper when he stopped.

Everything hurt.

It was like my brain was rebooting and each system it brought on line shut down as the pain receptors kicked in.

Ty crawled on top of me and licked the blood from my nose.

I tried not to gag cause it hurt too much.

"You really are going to taste special," he hummed and bared his fangs for another slick lick.

"Stop hitting on me," I groaned. "You're making me blush."

He bent in, and I shot a thin needle of force through his heart in a loud pop that echoed through the room.

One of the vampires gathered shrieked like a wounded animal and the rest joined the keening.

Maybe it was me screaming too as I shoved the disintegrating showboat off before he got ick all over my jacket and took out the rest of the group.

Except Claude.

Who stood by the door, his hand on the handle.

"Thank you Marshal, I am in your debt again."

He opened the door with a flourish and sped past the Normanii crawling on the ceiling to escape into the night.

Eric, Rollo and the other one raced down the stairs, swords drawn and stopped short as the bodies of the deceased vampires turned to ash and started drifting.

"You did all this alone?" Eric asked.

I made it to my elbows and knees, and then up on one foot.

"Don't everyone rush to help," I snapped.

A beautiful naked woman morphed from the Hund by his side and rushed to lend a hand.

I leaned a little harder than I needed and looked a little longer than I should have, if you could judge by the Viking's glare.

I didn't care.

I just won their fight and part of their argument for them.

He could cut me some slack or kiss my-

"We went to find you at the watcher's house," he grunted. "Someone has busted the wards and taken her."

I smacked my head and winced.

I'm an ass.

The wards would weaken with the old Marshal's death and I didn't do a damn thing to shore them up.

My fault.

"You should have-" Elvis started.

"I know, I know," I waved him off.

"If you knew, you should have stopped it," the Viking chided.

He was right, even if I didn't correct him.

I should have known.

"Let's go," I said and hobbled out.

Not before one last look at his Hund just before she shifted to her wolf form. Eric growled but I could swear she was smiling.

37

CHAPTER THIRTY FIVE

"War is starting Marshal."

"It's been going on forever," I reminded him.

"Aye," he agreed, then glanced over at the blond woman who was his Hund. I liked the tender look in his eye, the protective way he stared at her.

Maybe he was appreciating the curve of her pert bottom in the yoga pants.

I know I was.

"It's a different kind of war," he swiped his eyes over to catch me staring and was kind enough not to say anything about it. "I checked with the Jarl's and they've adjusted the threat level."

"Threat Level Midnight?"

He smiled, but it didn't touch his eyes.

"Threat Level Annihilate. The blood suckers have been around too long. We don't know who they have aligned themselves with this go round," he sighed. "But it's worse."

Which meant it was going to get a lot worse.

More innocent people were going to die.

And I was off on a witch hunt.

Literally.

"I wish I could join you," I told him.

"And I wish we had your magic by our side," Eric offered, a wistful tone in his voice. "We'll find more."

"Or make some."

He nodded and held out his hand.

"Good hunting," said the Normanii.

We used a traditional forearm grip and I felt the tingle of magic inside him. He was possessed, but the spirit wasn't evil. I gripped harder, and the took it as a challenge, tiny smirk turning up one corner of his mouth.

I sent out some feelers and got an impression.

He had a Viking warrior in his soul, an original Berserker cursed by an Indian Shaman up by Newfoundland almost a thousand years ago.

I sensed pain.

And hunger.

For vengeance. For justice. For freedom.

The Normanii nodded at me. He knew what I was feeling, what I was reading.

He would be hungry forever, or until the Vampires were eliminated, which was just as long as forever. They had been here since the beginning of time, feeding on the edge of humanity.

No reason to think a Shield wall would stop them permanently.

"But we'll protect them," he said as if reading my mind.

Guess I needed to work on my poker face.

"The sheep need protecting."

"And we're the wolves to do it."

"Wolves eat sheep."

"It's the idea behind the principle," he said.

That earned a smile from me.

"Luck be with you," I wished.

"It's better with you," he said. "I've got the strength of my blade, and just vampires to kill. You'll have to stop what the witchy women are doing."

He gave me another nod and I watched him walk over to join his werewolf. They linked fingers and trailed off toward the French Quarter and whatever undead needed killing on the streets there.

I stared at the cemetery in the direction of the River.

There was some bad mojo brewing up there. I could feel it swirling, like a vortex over the city, pulling in bad vibes, bad thoughts, bad feelings.

"He seemed like a nice guy," Elvis whispered near my ear.

I almost jumped in the water.

"You need to be scared," he continued, a serious look on his ghost face. "Another Watcher has been taken on your watch."

He didn't need to be a ghost to make me shiver at that.

The Vikings had a job to protect people from the predators that hunted for their blood at night. I had a job to protect the world.

And I was failing.

I messed up with my Watcher.

I wasn't about to let it happen with another.

"We better hurry," I told him and took off jogging to catch a Trolley car to the Cemetery.

He didn't have a choice to keep up.

38

CHAPTER THIRTY SIX

The second St. Louis Cemetery was smaller than the first, surrounded by the same white walls, populated with the same style of tombstone and mausoleums.

A historic preservation committee placed plaques on the walls, and changed the locks on the black iron gates every other year to keep vandals out.

They succeeded most of the time, but couldn't hold back the ravages of time.

Tombs that dated from the early 1800's dotted the landscape that too up most of an odd sized city block.

And the gates were open.

"Ready for this?" I asked myself as much as Elvis.

"I wish I had more to offer," he said.

"Just be prepared," I told him. "I can't communicate with the dead like you can."

"You didn't do such a great job with the living."

He was right.

I'd tried to make an alliance with Beth's Coven, but they didn't show up.

I couldn't blame them really. She was a weak witch, new to this world, and her Coven was the weakest in NOLA. Partnering with the Dixie Mafia was a desperation move, and my asking for their help made me feel all the more desperate.

I could have asked the Normanii for help, but the vampire conclave demanded their attention.

And Knu wouldn't interfere, or couldn't. I wasn't sure which was closer to the truth.

The fact that she shared so much with me about the Judge surprised me. I couldn't think about that now though. I needed my faith, my confidence.

It was just me against the witches and whatever monster they had conjured to Memphis and scattered to New Orleans.

I wished I had a Valkyrie by my side.

Fighting with my sister in law would have helped. She was one of the most powerful Battlemages I had ever known and her spell was the one that scattered these creatures to the wind.

She had done it to save me, to save us when we busted up the spell, and now she wasn't talking to me.

What do you do with a wizard who doesn't want to be found?

Especially one who dated Odin and who probably was hiding out in Valhalla even as I stood outside the wrought iron gates of a historic cemetery.

"Get in there scardy cat," I said under my voice.

"I can't move until you do," the ghost answered.

Each journey of a thousand miles begins with the first step. So, does each battle.

"Full Frontal!" I screamed and poofed into the middle of the cemetery.

Screw walking.

39

CHAPTER THIRTY SEVEN

"You came alone?" Gloria sneered. "You are a fool."

I blinked back the déjà vu and brought a spell to mind.

She stood in front of a raised stone tomb turned into an altar. Hannah was tied to it, passed out or ensorcelled. I couldn't tell which from here.

Gloria had the stone knife in one hand, and a closed fist with the other.

"Phyllis," she nodded.

The Voo Doo witch stepped out of the shadows and blew white powder into a cloud that drifted over my face.

"I've spent the last ten years building up a resistance to Iocane powder," I quipped, wiggled my fingers and knocked her out.

Guess the time for talk was over.

"Marshal," Elvis warned.

Then the demon stepped over her corpse.

It was a soul catcher, modelled on the scales of justice and based on the Greek goddess Themis. In some reliefs, she is pictured as a beautiful woman with justice on her mind.

In the one's we don't allow humans to see, she is a monster with large flat scale plates where her hand should be.

Guess which one showed up that night?

I caught a bit of luck though.

The ritual hadn't started.

A soul catcher needs souls, and setting the ritual in a place of the dead seemed like a bad idea.

The demon took a swing at my head and I ducked under the whistling plate.

"Marshal," Elvis called out again.

Gloria began chanting, raising the knife over her head and concentrating on a symbol carved in the stone of the tomb. A resurrection glyph.

Designed to bring back the dead.

Like the body of a thirty-thousand-year-old saber toothed tiger. Or the couple of thousand people buried in the cemetery.

A couple of thousand souls that would satiate even the most hungry demon soul catcher.

And make the witch her mastered it more powerful than ever.

The powder Phyllis blew lingered in a cloud and I could see the outlines of shapes in it. People shapes.

The demon lunged forward and I skittered a couple of force spells off its hide, which it was kind enough to ignore.

"Ghosts," shouted Elvis.

I vaulted over a burial vault and slid behind a mausoleum shaped like the Parthenon. It wasn't lost on me that I was hiding behind Greek reliefs modeled on the monster that chased me.

Gloria's voice grew higher as she started for the apex of the spell.

I figured I had ten seconds, maybe twelve.

"Cowabunga!" I whipped around the corner of the marble, shot a force of air straight into the soul catcher and knocked it back.

The wind circled around and lifted up the top of a tomb and I jumped on it like a surfboard, cruising straight for Gloria to disrupt the spell.

Phyllis shot me.

Literally.

With a gun.

What kind of witch brings a gun to a spell fight?

I felt the slug pound into my shirt and heard the shot as I careened off the slab and bounced off a tomb.

My divine wind died out and the marble cracked into a hundred pieces as it fell into another.

Phyllis stood up higher, and waved up the marble detritus and shot it toward me as I struggled to breath.

"Marshal!" Elvis called out.

"You keep saying that," I gasped.

I rolled down and out. The shower of razor sharp rock pinged into the wall I was just leaning against and rained down on me.

"Try to say it sooner!" I chastised the ghost.

"Like now?"

"Now?"

I didn't see him nod.

The Soul Catcher lashed out with a scale, caught me on the side and pounded me through the air to land in a heap on the other side of the cemetery.

Ouch.

I stood up, saw the knife start to fall and had just enough time to think a thought when Harold showed up.

Phyllis may have brought a gun to the fight.

I brought a two-ton saber tooth tiger.

Technically, I didn't bring him, but Beth and her Coven rode in like the cavalry.

They weren't much more than a distraction.

But Harold was the real deal.

He plowed into Gloria and knocked the Sidhe on her ass.

I would have cheered, but I was still having the whole trouble breathing thing. I managed a gasp though, so the thought was there.

Beth, Angie and one of the WWE women held Phyllis in a triangle of spells, each winging one at her one at a time while she held them off like a master in an old karate movie.

"At the same time!" I screamed instruction.

It came out as a wheeze.

Softer than a wheeze.

Gloria shrieked and sent a spell toward Harold. He sidestepped it and one of the Maine Coon Cats, two hundred pounds of feline slammed into her back.

I wanted to cheer again, but saved my breath and poofed back into the fight instead.

Three of the other Coven zapped the Soul Catcher with spells, but they weren't strong enough to do more than irritate it.

I heard a roar and turned to see Harold back away from Gloria with a long bloody gash in his flank.

The Maine coon Cat was down, looked like he was out of the fight forever.

Phyllis shot a spell into Angie and caught her of guard. The little witch went sprawling. Her collapse distracted Beth, who took a shot to the solar plexus that set her crashing back into a marble statue.

That was going to leave a mark.

The GLOW witch let out a banshee yell and rushed the Voo Doo woman. Phyllis screamed and cast out more of the powder in an expanding ring of wind.

It twirled among the tombs and swirled around the gathered spirits drawing them in until the air over the cemetery was heavy with the weight, like a pregnant storm cloud ready to downpour.

Gloria backed the Saber tooth into a corner and drew back her hand with a tiny black ball of energy, a death spell. The cat was trapped.

I zipped a spell and slapped her hand, caught up the black cloud and splashed it across the Soul Catcher.

It couldn't bellow, couldn't moan, couldn't make a sound as it arched up in agony and fell toward the alter.

I zinged Hannah up and away from the stone, smudging the ritual spell as I did, rendering it useless.

Hannah fetched up against the side of a marble sarcophagus. "Watch her Elvis."

The ghost shimmered over her to do what he could.

Gloria shrieked in rage and shot a wall of force into me. I planted my feet and redirected it, added my own and scooped up the cavalry Coven to lift them over the walls and out of harm's way.

"You think you've beaten me human?" Gloria gloated. "This changes nothing."

She windsurfed to the alter, and whisked Phyllis up and over toward her.

They reached the Soul Catcher at the same time.

I prepared a stall and stun spell to stop her from teleporting out.

She zigged when I thought she would zag.

Gloria stabbed Phyllis in the heart with the stone knife and sent up a shield around them.

Though I had destroyed the first ritual, the Sidhe had a backup.

She drained the essence from Phyllis and tapped into the demon trapped inside the Soul Catcher.

A sound like the wail of a woman tortured in hell echoed across the cemetery. The pain and anguish of the witch bound with the demon was heart wrenching and soul crushing.

Gloria extracted both of their life force into herself in one huge gulp of air.

"Be seeing you darling," she called out.

I sent a shot toward her but too late.

She had already disappeared.

40

CHAPTER THIRTY EIGHT

"Nothing from nothing leaves nothing," Elvis sang.

I stared at the empty space on the edge of the graveyard. Gloria was gone and so was the body of the Scales, the soul monster. Phyllis lay at odd angles, arms akimbo, head thrown back, mouth etched in a permanent scream I hope she carried into the afterlife.

I'd have to take her body to the Judge.

Hannah hobbled on wobbly legs and wrapped her fists around my biceps.

"That was...intense," she said in wonder, eyes glazed.

"We survived."

"Uh-huh," she reached up and pulled my lips to hers, planted soft wet kiss on mine.

After a moment, she stepped back, stronger now and a little more recovered and shook her head, like waking from a dream.

"My kisses can have that effect on people."

"NOLA man," she gave me a half grin. "Things great crazy up in the Big Easy."

A pair of headlights cut across the graveyard, a giant black Suburban that looked like a Hollywood movie version of secret government agency parking next to the gate.

"Trouble?" I asked.

Hannah shrugged.

"That starts with T, and that rhymes with D, and that stands for Done," the ghost chimed in.

"Any luck on that memory spell?"

She nodded, but didn't get the chance to say what kind of luck that might be. Pointed in the right direction, cure, or book sitting on the side of her sofa. Digby popped out of the back door of the SUV, flanked by a couple of walls of human flesh.

Seriously, where did they recruit these bodyguards? Ex-NFL combine players-R-US?

The trio weaved their way through the piles of dust, Digby smiling and concerned at the same time. His hair didn't have a strand out of place.

"Marshal," he chirped.

"Digby."

"Digby Richmond," he held out a hand to Hannah. "Damn glad to meet you."

"Hannah," she introduced herself.

"The Watcher, right? Did I get that right? I'm still learning about all of this."

"You're here Digby?"

The two mountains of meat shifted closer to their boss. Guess that came out a little harsher than I meant.

"Right, Daddy says I need to focus and stay on point better.

Always be improving, that's my motto. One of them, anyway. Dad says he can't hold off the authorities any longer. You have about five minutes before several departments descend on this place en masse."

"That was nice of him to warn me?"

"I know, right? Weird. You ever wake up to your Daddy one morning and realize he's got all this stuff up in his head and you just wish there was a way to scoop it out and put it in your own?"

"Gross," Hannah held her head. "I've had my fill of zombies."

Digby shivered.

"I didn't mean it so grotesque like that, but more like a knowledge transfer. I spent most of the past decade thinking Daddy was just a criminal and thug. Turns out, he's got a lot more going on than I thought."

"Three minutes," grunted the bodyguard on his right.

"Right. Got to go, Marshal."

Digby held out his hand and shook mine, then Hannah's again. The duo began to escort him back toward the SUV, when hell broke loose.

It was in the form of flashing lights and roaring engines, all sliding to a stop around the entrances to the graveyard. A helicopter thumped in the distance, sound growing louder as a spotlight danced across the pavement searching its way toward the headstones.

"Is your watch slow Digby?"

He held it up and glanced at the silver face, shrugged.

I extended the thought and poofed us all a couple hundred yards away in a blink.

Teleporting. Movement at the speed of thought. It's incredible when you have a ton of power to do it. Not so much when it's unexpected.

I was ready for it.

No one else was.

Hannah collapsed in the street with a shriek as she lost her balance. The left bodyguard bent over and threw up his lunch into the gutter. The right one fainted. Only Digby seemed unaffected.

"That was so awesome!" he squealed.

We could see the strobing lights outside the graveyard up the street. We were outside of a perimeter that law enforcement established, so we were safe.

"Hey man, hey man," a small tour group bustled over to us. "That was some cool magic! Can you do that again?"

"I saw someone do that in Vegas," sniffed another in a haughty voice.

"Street magicians are bums," another muttered.

"No man, right out of nowhere. Bam!"

Hannah climbed up and found her street legs again.

"Body?" Elvis whispered in my ear.

Crap. We forgot the witch inside the fence. The cops were going to stumble over it any second, and then things would get complicated.

"You steady?" I took Hannah by the shoulders. "Can you make it home?"

She nodded.

I turned to Digby.

"They're going to have questions about your truck."

He waved it off.

"Daddy will take care of it."

"Hey man, do something else," one of the tourists clamored.

I stuck my hand in my coat pocket.

"Pick a card," I told him and jerked my hand in the air with a shower of sparks.

I poofed while they were distracted.

Over the body in the cemetery. At least I got the location right.

"Freeze! Don't move!" I looked over at a rookie cop, gun shaking in his hand as he aimed it in panicked terror.

"Hands in the air," he screamed again.

"You said don't move."

He pulled the trigger. I watched his finger go white on the metal. This was going to hurt.

We appeared in front of the Judge just as the bullet him my Kevlar laced tee shirt. I plopped over backwards on the hewn stone floor of his chambers, and landed on the stiffening body of the witch.

"You couldn't have done that a second sooner?" I groaned and rubbed my sternum as I got up. Pain radiated from my lower left ribcage, and I could tell it was going to bruise.

The tee shirt was designed to stop penetration from bullets, claws and anything that tried to get inside my skin to the tender bits and morsels. The magic and Kevlar weave could do that, but the force of the blow still had to be dispersed somehow, and I hadn't figured out the magic of the quantum physics yet to redirect it.

For now, it manifested as pain. Lots of pain.

But at least I wasn't leaking.

I crawled to my feet and stared at the Judge as he sat in his stand. I could see now that it was modeled on a throne, and once your eyes are open to something, you can't unsee it. It looked pre-Celtic in origin, an ancient design that probably served as a daily reminder of what he had to do to get his power.

He stared at me with overlarge eyes from behind the round spectacles and didn't speak.

I didn't say a word, just nudged the dead witch closer to him.

I could still see the ghost of an image on his face, the general he had been in the past. But a dozen thousand years tend to make you look different.

I supposed only because he did indeed look different.

An old man, no, older than I had even imagined. A wizard who had seen more death than anyone save the Grim Reaper himself, if he was indeed real.

If there were dragons, and gnomes and leprechauns, I suppose there was a harbinger of death, perhaps even one of the four horsemen of legend.

He sighed.

It hurt me to hear it.

So much pain in that sigh, so much pity, all directed at me. The Gnome could see the future.

I suspected the Judge planned it.

Shaped it.

Set the inevitable upon its course and sat back.

Not like some uncaring god playing with the lives of mortals. More like a guardian who stood at a gate, holding back the forces of evil.

I'd been to War before.

I know what it can do to a man's mind, even one made strong by magic.

Constant battle makes a soul weary, or worse yet, the quantum aspect of battle changes the very nature of the soul. Exposure to the worst things in the Universe, the most vile and evil things man can imagine or not change the very nature of the magic we have inside each of us.

Positive thoughts yield a positive life. It's quantum.

Negative thoughts must therefore yield a negative life.

It let me return his gaze, and reverse the pity.

He shook his head.

Like speaking to a kid.

A sharp kid, smart and knowledgeable, but in the way only those who read books can tell you about the Sistine Chapel. They know of it, but do not know it.

That's how he looked at me.

Like he had a secret he couldn't share because I wasn't ready for it.

"Are you ready?" he said in a midwestern American accent, still sounding like the Colonel from MASH. "Saddle up."

He raised a finger and pointed.

"Why didn't you tell me?" I called out before he pulled the poof on me.

There it was.

Another sad look.

He blinked and I knew.

Like he put the thought in my head, and as soon as I thought that, I knew he had.

He wanted to tell me but was afraid. Afraid it would break me. Afraid I wasn't strong enough.

He knew the road ahead of me, knew where it ended, how it ended and even though he wanted to help, he could not.

Or rather, he was helping, but in ways I couldn't see, didn't know.

But I was strong enough for it.

The longest lasting Marshal he'd ever trained.

Not the most talented, though he could have left that thought out.

But certainly, the most tenacious, and clever and resourceful. And lucky. Damn lucky.

He made me think all of those things, let me know that's how he felt, all in the blink of an eye, an epiphany that filled me with a sense of confidence.

Then poof he was gone.

41

CHAPTER THIRTY NINE

Poof.

Or rather I was.

"Damn it," I said. "You would think that he would poof me where I needed to do the work. Something like Four Corners or the edge of the Navajo reservation. Why would he send me back to New Orleans by the river?"

"Don't scream so loud, he'll hear you," said Elvis.

"I don't care if he can hear me. He's supposed to be the most powerful wizard on Earth and we're up against a deadline. But he doesn't send me any closer to the action. It doesn't make sense."

"Maybe he wants us to take the train."

"That I could understand," I screamed at the ghost. "But if that were true why didn't he put us at the train station."

I heard an insect hum and looked up to see a dot on the

horizon.

"If that's a dragon I'm going home."

It wasn't a dragon, or if it was it was the most erratic flying dragon I've ever heard about. I'd ever never actually seen a dragon, so could only relate what the tales had told. Whatever this was weaved through the sky like a bumblebee

As it got closer I saw two wings and heard what sounded like a lawn mower engine. I wasn't going home. But I think I found how the judge wanted us to get to the Southwest.

The plane lined up on the levy, cut the engine and glided into a shallow stop on the short grass. A little man hopped out of the rear seat and walk straight up to me.

"Marshall?" He had a funny accent I couldn't place and I realized why when he pulled the goggles up off his grease stained face. Another gnome.

"I am," I told him.

"Sister said you might need a ride," he gave me an exaggerated wink.

"Sister?"

"Our medium. She said to meet you here and give you a ride wherever you needed to go. I'm all gassed up and ready to fly."

"Are you sure that thing is safe?" Elvis asked.

"You're a ghost," I reminded him. "What are you worried about?"

He floated over to inspect the plane, thin fabric over metal struts and a small engine at the front twirling a wooden propeller. It looked more like a toy than an aircraft.

"I wonder why he didn't send a Lear?"

"She knows I don't have one of those," said the gnome pilot. "I built this one myself with my own hands in my shed."

I didn't want to tell the poor creature that it looked like it.

"Ready," he said and invited us to the contraption with a flourish of his hands.

"As we'll ever be."

I trudged to the plane and let the pity wash up for a moment. On a commercial flight, I could have taken a nap. I didn't think my sphincter would relax enough in this plane to let me breathe, let alone sleep.

The gnome hopped in the back, and stepped on the wing to climb in the front bucket.

"Careful," he called out as he dropped giant bug-eyed goggles over his eyes. "Don't' want to hurt the wing. We need that to fly."

"Wings and prayers," I settled in and buckled up.

"Those help too!" he called out, spun the end of the plane around and gunned it for the river.

It was probably Elvis screaming during the whole take off.

THE END